GREENI

A Commander Shaw novel

Philip McCutchan

Hodder & Stoughton
LONDON SYDNEY AUCKLAND TORONTO

British Library Cataloguing in Publication Data
McCutchan, Philip
  Greenfly : a Commander Shaw novel.
  I. Title
  823'.914[F]   PR6063.A167

  ISBN–0–340–40193–1

Hodder and Stoughton Editorial Office: 47 Bedford Square, London WC1B 3DP.

1

I was wearing thick woollen gloves but even so my fingers, after a couple of hours or so of scanning the not-so-distant frontier, seemed frozen to the leather-covered metal of my binoculars, powerful ones and very heavy. My whole body was stiff with the cold as I lay there between the thickly-growing pines. Snow lay over the trees and everything was very still and quiet: it was lonely in the Harz Mountains, very lonely and my nerves were on edge as I waited for something to develop, waited and scanned the border below me, the wire and the minefields and the ingenious traps along the frontier with East Germany. I could see the occasional patrol carried out by the East German troops and once I believed I made out a Russian uniform, a man of the Red Army standing for a moment in the cold outside the frontier post. If the Russians were there, it wasn't too good: something could have leaked. There was always room for leaks, far too much room. These days security had become a joke, largely. There was always a mole and you could seldom trust anybody.

I thought of what Hans Schulz had said last night, down in Braunlage – Hans, one of our 6D2 West Germany operatives, had put me up overnight after I'd driven through from Hanover. We'd drunk beer together with his wife and son, drunk it out of old tankards with lids and glass bottoms, and he'd remarked on the latter.

"We have them too," I said.

"Yes. And for the same purpose." Hans, a big man with thick grey hair and a bushy beard, got to his feet and went over to a window. "To watch for the enemy . . . the sudden thrust of a knife or the lifting of a flintlock, in those old days. Now we have more to watch for, *hein?*"

"Dead right," I said, and felt more than ever uneasy because of his tone.

"This will not be easy."

"I know that."

"The Ladybirds will kill."

"I know that too – of course they'll kill, that's what they're there for."

"But I mean more than that, my friend!" Hans lumbered away from the window and stood with his back to the blazing coal fire. "They will kill their own, do you not see, if there is danger, they will kill rather than that anyone be questioned by the KGB."

That hadn't in fact surprised me: back in Focal House in London, Max had said much the same thing. But in that room in Braunlage, a room lit only dimly so that the great body of Hans Schulz was outlined against the glow of the coal and the flickering flames so that he appeared like some grotesque ogre out of Germany's past, the words sent a shiver down my spine as though Hans Schulz had peered ahead into the future and had seen its shape. The Harz Mountains that straddled the fringe of the Iron Curtain were a region of splendour but also of deep gloom. Many legends of popular Teutonic folklore had been woven around The Rosstrappe, Brocken, Teufelsmauer, Hexen-tanzplatz . . . Brocken's summit, often shrouded in mist, was said to house the Spectre of Brocken, though in truth he might have been no more than a whorl of the mist itself.

And the close-set pines, among which currently I lay. I had always found conifers depressing. It was just as I came to a kind of peak of depression and unease that I heard the faint sound from behind me and then, a fraction of a second later, heard the shooting start on the western side of the frontier.

★

I'd dropped into all this little more than a week earlier, when I'd got back from a job in Spain and was expecting to be sent on a month's leave. Felicity Mandrake was going to spend that leave with me and to hell with what Max, who was head of 6D2 Britain, thought about it – Max could be stuffy when his field men and women got emotionally involved, but both Felicity and I reckoned we were mature enough to distinguish between duty and the other thing. Anyway, when I got to my flat I found it had been done over, and very, very thoroughly. So thoroughly that it was almost impossible to say if anything had been taken, but I didn't believe it had after I'd done a quick check on valuables. Robbery didn't appear to be the motive, so what was? Someone with a very deep grudge, I decided when I found my telephone hidden beneath an upturned arm chair with the receiver off the handset. I heard sounds as I picked it up and I listened: a nasal voice was giving me the time and it wasn't British time – it was hours out. After a moment I realised I was listening to the New York Speaking Clock. At around 80p a minute at peak times, that could be rocketing my telephone bill; I shoved the receiver back on the rest pronto. It was a very dirty trick and in a flat fury I ran through my list of enemies. I couldn't think of any personal ones likely to be so vindictive so assumed this was business, in which case Max could be persuaded to put it on expenses, or so I hoped.

I started a search for clues.

In 6D2, when this sort of thing happens, we don't call in the police. We prefer not to involve them unless it becomes inevitable, and that's the way the British Government, and all other governments who give their approval to our activities, want it too. We are international but we are undercover, ostensibly a fact-finding agency with contacts in all kinds of places high and low almost world wide, and we have background government support – we've often, very often, been useful to governments. They don't like doing their own dirty work if it can be avoided, though I use the word 'dirty' not in any pejorative sense since we always strive for cleanliness in thought and deed – in other words, we're on the Right Side. I made my search with due care, using gloves and a delicate touch, and I found nothing. Nothing, that was, until my telephone rang. I answered it and an unknown male voice said, "Commander Shaw?"

"Yes," I said.

"The clock has been speaking since just before midnight six days ago."

"You bastard," I said.

"Yes." There was something like a chortle. "Pick up the telephone, and look at its under side." Then my caller rang off. I wasn't going to risk activating a possible booby trap by turning the instrument upside down, but I didn't need to: I'd put it down on a glass-topped coffee table, miraculously unbroken, when I'd rescued it from beneath the arm chair, and I had simply to look up from below. I saw a sticker, a piece of white self-adhesive plastic with a thing like a beetle on it, coloured green. Carefully I lifted the telephone and peeled off the sticker, wrapped it in a ten pound note, and put it in my pocket-book.

Then I left the flat and headed for Focal House, fast.

"Clever," Max said, and grinned. I felt like murder. He went on thoughtfully, "Six days. Let's see." He fiddled with his calculator. "At an average charge of, say, 70p a minute, it comes to a little over six thousand pounds. Someone doesn't like you."

"Quite," I said. "And I'm passing the bill to accounts."

"Why?" Max looked up. "You get a damn good expense account of your own, don't you?"

"Adequate for most things, not this."

"We'll go into it later," Max said equably. I believe he was still amused. He sat there like God, which in a sense he was to those who worked for 6D2, God of Focal House and the whole set-up in Britain, which was a big one. Max carried immense authority in his person and he looked like a resurrection of a World War Two admiral, direct, penetrating eyes, pugnacious jaw, beetling brows, almost a caricature of the species. He jabbed at the sticker, still lying on its ten pound note. "This convey anything?"

I shook my head and lit a cigarette after offering one to Max, who declined: he preferred his own brand which cost a fortune. "Not to me. I know nothing of beetles."

"Not a beetle, Shaw, a greenfly."

"Really."

"Hemiptera-Homoptera. Bugs. Parthenogenetic reproduction – breed very fast as a result. Soft skinned, three-jointed suctorial beak, long antennae, two-jointed feet – "

"And all that has been drawn?"

Max said, "No. The thing's rudimentary. But it's interesting." He gave me a direct look. "No connection with anything or anyone from the past – in your experience?"

"None."

"Then who do you think is responsible?"

I said, "With no evidence to go on, I suspect WUS-WIPP." The reference, as Max knew well enough, was to the outfit known as World Union of Socialist Scientific Workers for International Progress in Peace. They were certainly international but the peace part was sheer boloney: WUSWIPP were killers and fanatics for disrupting anything that held any potential at all for peaceful co-existence, to dig up an old phrase from the past. WUS-WIPP and I had clashed so many times I'd lost count; and because I'd been reasonably successful against them they hated my guts. That lengthy long-distance telephone call fitted. I said as much to Max.

"You didn't recognise the voice, you said."

"Right, I didn't. There's no evidence in that." Nor had I picked up an accent. The voice had been flat, toneless. "No indication of nationality though it didn't strike me the man was speaking his own language."

"And no forced entry – front door and windows intact."

9

I shrugged. "It's easy enough to use a skeleton key."

"In your case two skeleton keys – Yale and mortice, but I agree it's easily done. What do you think they were after, Shaw?"

I said I had no idea. From time to time I had taken papers home for study, but never anything with a high security classification, and while I had been away in Spain I'd left nothing documentary in the flat: my safe, of which the intruders had bust the combination, had been empty. But the fact that the safe had been opened could suggest a search for documents as I admitted to Max.

"Exactly." There was accusation in the tone.

"I've never – "

"Yes, all right, Shaw. I know you're not a damn fool."

"Thank you for that," I said a little tartly. "If it was that – "

"They drew a blank. But it makes me think. It makes me think this: that they, whoever they were and for now let's call them the greenflies, believed you *might* have had something worth getting their hands on."

"Such as – in particular?"

Max spread his hands and shrugged massive shoulders. "You're known – probably – to be one of our top field men. WUSWIPP knows that for sure. Others may know it too. Modern bushels conceal very little light."

"You're not answering the question," I said, and Max gave a grin. He said he knew he wasn't, because he didn't know what the answer was; but it seemed he had a theory.

He said musingly, "Greenfly. Things eat them, prey on them."

"Nature," I said. "Everything preys on something. I imagine greenfly eat some lesser species, don't they?"

Max said no, they didn't. They ate plants as any gardener could testify. He said I'd better have a word with Arthur Webb, who wasn't a gardener but the top man in 6D2 HQ London on Russian affairs, the head of the Iron Curtain desk. I asked what the connection was, but Max simply picked up his internal line and got Arthur Webb and said I'd be right down.

Max's office suite, the last word in luxury, occupied the whole of the penthouse and looked out across the helicopter landing pad over all London and part of four counties. Arthur Webb was five floors down from the suite; I descended in the lift past accounts, medical section, labs and analysis, fingerprints, weapons' section, finance, industrial counter-espionage . . . even the lift was luxury, beautifully panelled in bird's-eye maple. 6D2 drew its ample funds from many sources, big business from all over plus grants from a number of governments who nevertheless refrained from any interference and kept themselves strictly in the background. We had all the scope we wanted and our name stood high. Of individual names none were more trusted than Arthur Webb: he was integrity personified and he had a long experience of affairs on the other side of the Iron Curtain, right back in fact to the end of World War Two. As regards Russia itself he had seen them all come and go: Stalin, Bulganin, Khruschev, Kosygin . . . Brezhnev, Chernenko, Andropov, now Gorbachev. Once, he had been on the Russian desk in the Foreign Office and since leaving the FO he had been infiltrated into Russia on a number of occasions, ostensibly trade mission ones. He was getting on now, he must have been around sixty-four and looked it: thin white hair, dessicated flesh, a stoop, exaggerated because he was a tall man, only an inch below my own height; but he was all there mentally, sharp and with-it as ever.

He asked, when I'd sat down, "What's all this about?"

I said, "Greenfly, I think."

He looked at me sharply and said, "Ha. Start at the beginning, please, Commander."

Somehow, that 'ha' told me I wouldn't be wasting my time. I gave him the facts briefly; he nodded at intervals, keeping his gaze on my face. I ended by saying that Max seemed to have found some significance in the depiction of the greenfly.

Webb said, "Yes. He could be right. It's stretching it a little, but it could connect." He went off at a tangent. "You've been in Spain – am I right? How long?"

"Three weeks, just over. The Costa del Sol job."

"Yes, yes. Out of touch. Things move fast these days."

I said, "If what you're getting at blew up while I was in Spain, then whoever broke into my flat wouldn't have been looking for any documents in connection with it. I know I'm not world famous, but my intruders must have known my movements."

"Oh, of course." Webb brushed that aside. "What I'm getting at as you put it – it has its origins rather farther back than three weeks. I'll be brief, Commander: there's a person coming through."

"Through the Curtain?"

"Yes. A woman. We don't know her name. We've simply received word that she's coming through within the next four days." Webb shook his head and pulled at his chin. "I confess I don't like it at all. There's an amateurish ring. If only we could have handled this right through ourselves – but that wasn't to be." He gave me a sharp look. "She wants a pick-up."

"Where?"

"Harz Mountains in West Germany. Near Braunlage."

I laughed. "The frontier's not passable!"

"Ah, but it's been crossed quite a number of times in point of fact, though in normal circumstances I'd agree . . . minefields, electrified wire, booby traps, guards and patrols – they do keep 'em in! But again that amateur aspect, you see – all those successful crossings by unorthodox means, I have to admit they've all been made by amateurs, ordinary people trying to get the hell out."

"And this time?"

Webb said, "Oh, it's covered. Hans Schulz, our man on the spot. He'll assist."

"When is this to happen?" I asked.

"As I said, within the next four days. We await a positive time. And if you're going to ask what the special importance is, I'll tell you what we know, which in fact isn't much: the woman is coming through with information said to be vital to international peace. Because of the background, this is being taken very seriously indeed and we're in close consultation with – with the highest level in Whitehall."

"And the background?"

Webb smiled, put his finger-tips together and rested his chin on them. He went off at another tangent. "We were going to send Layton for the pick-up. But I wonder if you'd care to go instead?"

I said promptly, "When I've sorted out my flat, I'm going on leave."

"Why not postpone it? I can fix this with Max very easily in the circumstances."

"What circumstances for heaven's sake?"

Webb said, "The woman is one of a group calling themselves – I translate from the Russian – the Ladybirds." He added, as he probably noted the various expressions chasing themselves across my face, "Ladybirds prey on greenfly. I thought you'd be interested. Do you see a possible connection?"

I knew I'd lost my leave; Max would never let me off this particular hook. And come to that, I wouldn't mind the opportunity of making that six thousand quid genuinely expense deductible.

2

I had a long session with Arthur Webb. I wasn't familiar with the Harz Mountains or their contiguous areas of West Germany and he filled me in on detail. Also, he told me more about the Ladybirds: in Russia they were dissidents, always on the run from the KGB. They were liberal minded and they were mainly women, hence the cover name. The identity of the woman coming through was not known; in fact not much was known about the group as a whole, but a month or so earlier there had been a reference to them in a despatch from the British Embassy in Moscow. A woman had been shot and killed in the Naberezhnaya Morisa Toreza, outside the Embassy itself and before she had died and been dragged away she had shouted out something in English, something about wanting asylum. All this, Webb said, had been in the English press, but of course no explanation had ever come through from the Kremlin or the Soviet Embassy in London. The despatch from the Ambassador had indicated a belief that the woman had been a member of the Ladybirds, of whom his security section had picked up fragmentary reports over the last six months or so. They were being a nuisance to the Soviet authorities, who were doing their best not to admit their existence. Possibly more than a nuisance: there had been minor but expensive acts of sabotage in various parts of the Soviet Union, factories blown up, agricultural machinery damaged, that sort of thing. Killings as well: a troop convoy heading for Poland had been ambushed and assaulted with primitive petrol bombs. The soldiers had opened fire and a

14

number of women had been shot. These facts had permeated through to the Embassy in dribs and drabs and had been referred to in earlier reports to Whitehall and these reports had now been collated and the Ladybirds noted as the possible saboteurs.

I asked Arthur Webb where the report had come from as to the expected woman.

He said, "Radley-Bewick." Piers Radley-Bewick was our man in Moscow: the British public, and the Soviet authorities, knew him as a spy who'd fled to the East just before being arrested for ostensibly passing highly-classified material to the Russian Embassy, material to do with the British capacity to wage bacteriological warfare. Only a handful of people in Whitehall knew that the material was fairly useless but Radley-Bewick, a brave man and a patriot, was a valuable plant inside Russia once he had been allowed to make his getaway from Britain. One day, if he was lucky, he might be exchanged for a Russian held in this country. There was no guarantee that he would be lucky.

I asked, "Didn't he have anything else to offer? For instance, didn't he know what this vital piece of information is?"

"Apparently not. You know how it is, Commander. He may be trusted by the Russians, but he's always at risk just the same."

"These Ladybirds wouldn't chance it, in case he was ever pulled in by the KGB?"

"That's it," Webb said. "Or anyway, that's my assessment."

A reasonable one, I thought. No-one really trusts spies, not even the spy-masters. Such as Radley-Bewick live out their lives on a tight-rope. He had his ways of passing reports through to Focal House – not via the Embassy, who couldn't afford to be involved in espionage, which was why he'd been given to us by Whitehall in the first place, but by other means. We have a system of messengers, collection agents, commuting by air between most

15

parts of the world . . . Radley-Bewick would have used dead letter boxes and so on, casual bumpings in the street when a message could be passed, and never the same place or the same person twice. But I could understand that a dissident group inside Russia might prefer to keep their own counsel in certain circumstances.

After leaving Webb's office I went back to the penthouse suite and bearded Max. I said I wanted Miss Mandrake with me: she had been due to share that postponed leave, so she wouldn't have been re-allocated. Max didn't argue; he knew that in fact Felicity and I worked well together and never mind the emotional angle. But he was ungracious about it as usual and I knew he was envious: Felicity was a very attractive girl and Max had always had an eye for her though conscience and duty, and his own position as God in 6D2 HQ Britain, had kept a rigid control. Like the captain of a liner, all could sin save he. When I left Focal House I rang Felicity.

"Meet me at Martinez," I said. "Soonest possible. An early lunch. Bring an overnight bag." I rang off before the protests came: she would have understood that the leave was off. We'd been bound for the sunshine in Madeira . . .

London was grey and depressing, cold and about to rain, heavy cloud lying overall. Martinez would remind us of recent sunnier skies in Andalusia. I took a taxi to Regent Street and walked through to Swallow Street, ordered a large Scotch in the tiled bar and waited for it to be brought by the Spanish waiter. I asked for the menu: Felicity liked paella, I went for riñones Jerezano even though the Jerezano might not mix with the Scotch. Felicity arrived looking ruffled and drank a La Ina; she didn't say much, waited for me to tell her the score, which, in the bar, I didn't. We went up to the restaurant; the head waiter knew me and led us to a table for two in a corner where we were nicely distant from the other customers. I ordered;

when the waiter had gone Felicity asked what it was all about.

I said, "For a start, my flat's been done over." I told her about that and she was concerned and upset: a lot of the decor and furnishings had been her ideas, especially the bedroom. I didn't tell her much else, not there and then. "1355, Heathrow for Hanover," I added. "And I'm sorry about Madeira. Don't let it spoil your appetite, though. Good food costs money . . ." I was still sore about that six thousand pounds, the potential payer of which I still hadn't sorted out for dead certain. Felicity too had been rocked by that: there were all sorts of horrid implications. She had two small nephews who sometimes stayed with her. If ever they got to hear, they might see it as a hell of a joke to play on auntie. When we were in a taxi en route for Heathrow – I'd taken my grip to Focal House, not having intended camping out in my wrecked flat – I gave her such facts as I'd been told. My orders, I said, were to get to Braunlage and Hans Schulz, the 6D2 local agent who would give us all the assistance we needed. It was to his house that word would go, as soon as it reached Focal House, as to the time of the crossing from east to west. Once I'd contacted the woman, I was to extract the information from her and bring her to Focal House pronto.

"A short enough assignment," I said. Felicity gave a rather hollow laugh at that; I'd made similar remarks on earlier occasions. At Heathrow, we just about made it: Max himself had rung through and made it plain that we were to be given seats no matter who had to be bumped off to make room for us and if by any chance we were late the flight was to be held. We didn't talk much on the way but enjoyed another meal and a couple of large Scotches and touched down at Hanover at 1615 local time. It was snowing when we got there; I left Felicity drinking coffee in a café near the British Airways desk while I coped with the formalities involved in taking over the self-drive hire car, a Volkswagen, that had been fixed for me from Focal

17

House. As soon as I'd taken delivery we drove away from the airport, heading south for the Harz Mountains via Hildesheim and Salzgitter. By the time we reached Braunlage it was well past dark and the lights shining from the windows of the houses onto the lying snow – that and the pines rising up the sides of the massive Wurmberg above the small town – gave the place a fairyland look of Christmas and you half expected to meet a reindeer with sledge around the next corner. The feel of Christmas evaporated fast when I thought of the East German border not so far away.

I had been given detailed directions by Arthur Webb and I found Hans Schulz' house easily enough. Braunlage itself was built in a big clearing of the forest but the Schulz house was outside the town itself, closer to the mountains and the border, all by itself at the end of a rough track in another, smaller clearing beyond which close-set pines could be seen in my headlights as I approached. I had seen a bearded face peering from a lighted window as the Volkswagen crunched up the track and it was Schulz himself who opened the door even before I had tugged at the bell-pull.

"Herr Schulz?" I asked.

"*Ja.*"

"From Max," I said, and held out my 6D2 pass in the palm of my hand. Schulz nodded, stood aside, and told us to come in. His family was grouped around a blazing fire – the wife and two sons, whom he introduced. "They know my work," he said in English. "They are to be trusted. You may speak freely."

"All right," I said, though with inward misgivings: I'd been trained to a higher degree of security than this and talking to too many strangers can be a risk. However, this time I had to accept it; and it was a straightforward enough job, the taking over of a dissident when she arrived: the risks were all hers. I asked, "Have you any further information, Herr Schulz?"

"No, none. Like you, I wait."

"Yes," I said, and went on carefully, since I didn't yet know precisely how far Schulz took his wife and sons into his work details, "In London, I was told there would be . . . help."

"The diversion, yes. That I shall see to, with my sons."

I asked, "How will you know when to divert?"

Schulz smiled, and met his sons' eyes. "There will be a message, Commander."

"May I know who from, and how?"

"I think not. Not now. Later, yes."

I had to be content with that, but my mind roved over many possibilities and impossibilities. How on God's earth did one get an immediate message across the East German border other than perhaps by some sort of short-range radio contact, one that would surely be picked up – though perhaps, with a lot of luck, not pinpointed? One short transmission: It was possible. But there were all kinds of risks and somehow I couldn't see the Ladybirds chancing any radio transmissions. Schulz seemed disinclined at first to talk any more shop and we chatted about the London scene; he knew London quite well, having worked for a wine company in the West End back in the 'sixties, selling German wines. He was an unlikely-looking wine salesman; I would have put him down more as something like a forester or a game warden. Since those days he had paid only short visits and had found them depressing: London had changed. It was dirty, he said without apology, and there was no discipline anywhere, and the British roads were appalling. He didn't mean the state of upkeep, he meant the standard of driving.

"So dangerous," he said. "So many fools, and there is the lack of driving discipline. Here in Germany, the driving laws are obeyed by all but the tourists."

"You're a disciplined people," I said. I thought about Hitler, and before him the Kaiser. The people had had hard lessons in discipline right enough. But I took his point, and I appreciated it too – we could do with something of his ideas in Britain. I'd noticed when I'd been in Germany before how clean and tidy all the small towns were and I'd been told that the law made householders keep their gardens in good order, for one thing; there was none of the scruffy dereliction so evident in any English town's less fashionable quarter, the unkempt plots, the uncut grass, the bangers parked in the driveways of what had once been biggish houses now converted into flats. That, and the litter. I'd also seen how in Germany the pedestrians obeyed the little red and green men at the crossings even when there was no traffic in sight. While we talked, Schulz brought out the tankards and poured lager, which he called beer, and got back onto the subject of the Ladybirds, making the remark that they would kill whenever necessary. They sounded rather fearsome women. I didn't say anything to Schulz about the greenfly or what had happened to my flat. I didn't see that as his concern. Once he had assisted our female dissident across the border his part would have been played.

I did a little more probing about the frontier: Schulz had drunk a fair amount of good strong beer and had relaxed a little more. He said the woman would have a very good chance, though sooner her than him. The Harz Mountains formed a tough area physically, geographically, which was one reason why it had been chosen apparently – since it was not a good crossing point, and in fact there had never, so Schulz said, been an escape attempt made in the vicinity, the watch tended to be rather more lax than elsewhere. Another reason for the choice was that some essential maintenance work was going on, and was suffering delays on account of the wintry weather – sections of the fences being replaced, the ground being dug up . . . it was even believed likely that the electrification would be found switched off though this couldn't be entirely relied upon. What was certain, Schulz told me, was that there were no SM70s along the sector to be used; and the SM70, which scattered wicked little slivers of razor-sharp steel over a wide area, was regarded by escapers as the most terrible of all the border devices.

"A good chance," Schulz said again. But I wasn't sure that he wasn't deceiving himself.

When the time came for bed, Schulz showed me to my room while Frau Schulz showed Felicity to another. No hanky-panky: we were obviously not husband and wife. German discipline held even in the bedroom. If, that night, I'd attempted any wandering and been caught, the wrath of all the Teutonic gods would have fallen on me . . .

I lay awake: it could have been frustration. But I don't think it was. I believed something had woken me up, some small sound in the otherwise deadly silent night. Lying almost without breathing, and feeling an unusual prickle of apprehension running along my spine, I heard another sound, a creak of the stairs; then another. A shaft of moonlight showed behind the curtain over the window: the night had cleared, the snow-clouds gone. I saw in my imagination the tall trees, the thickness of the forest that covered the Harz Mountains, and I wondered what might have come through those trees to bring sounds to Schulz' house. After the two stair-creaks there was another silence. It lasted perhaps three minutes and then there was a tap at my door, which opened to admit candlelight, and I almost fell out of bed, seeing ghosts and worse: it could have been Felicity, taking a big risk of being burned at the stake as a fallen woman.

But it was Schulz, candle held high.

"Commander, are you awake?"

I said I was; I'd heard vague sounds, I said.

"Then you will get up, please. The message has come."

"The woman?"

"She will cross the frontier during the morning early, after the dawn patrol has withdrawn. I will guide you and then leave you."

To create his diversion, I supposed. I said, "Ready and willing, that's me. Have you woken Miss Mandrake?"

"It is not woman's work tonight," he answered, looking more than ever ogrish behind the candle's yellow light. I didn't argue; in fact I agreed with him, even though it was a woman that was coming over – I didn't want to risk Felicity so close to the border as I was going to be before long and I'd brought her for other reasons: she could be a help with the female dissident once I got her here to Schulz' house. The Ladybird might be more willing to talk to another woman than to me, and Arthur Webb had been specific that she was to be persuaded to talk, presumably just in case she was got at before she reached London. It was certain that once the East Germans or their Russian bosses knew that the border had been breached they might put two and two together and suspect a Ladybird and all their undercover operatives around the Harz and all the way to London would be alerted to go in for the elimination.

I got dressed: Schulz was already in his cold-weather rig, heavy boots, roll-top pullover, thick quilted anorak with hood, and over his arm he had similar gear for me. Also he had two torches, powerful ones, big jobs like those used aboard oil-tankers to look down the cargo tanks, and two pairs of binoculars. On the way out he collected a dismantled and cased sub-machine gun; the two sons brought similar weapons plus a sack that they told me contained grenades. As for me, I had my Colt Detective Special, a heavy job – 21 ounces, 6¾ inches, .38 calibre. Thus equipped, we left stealthily, like burglars, crunching through the snow and heading into the trees behind Hans Schulz who moved very purposefully, knowing his terrain, probably, like the back of his hand. I went behind him, with the sons in rear, like warders. We were soon climbing, shallow at first but growing steeper, and from time to time, in the moonlight, I could see Braunlage getting smaller below me. There were few lights showing that I could see; the little town slept the winter night away. I wondered they could sleep so easily, so close to the Iron Curtain's fringe. No doubt they'd grown used to it over the last forty-odd years, but they must have known that if ever the Russian armour rolled again, their little town would be among the first to be over-run.

Hans Schulz and the two sons moved with very little sound: they were well used to the forest. I was rather more clumsy and found it hard not to swear aloud when branches whipped across my face or the undergrowth caught my feet and tripped me. I fell once or twice, but each time the leading son took me from behind before I hit the ground. Moving on, climbing, beginning to feel warmer with the physical effort, I thought about Felicity alone in the Braunlage house with Schulz' wife. Frau Schulz had struck me as tough, a real German *hausfrau* with a granite jaw. She would be a good watchdog in Schulz' absence should any elements from the other side, men would could have come to know Schulz' associations, try anything nasty. As for my Miss Mandrake, she had steel in her as well. But worry still nagged. I didn't want anything to happen to her.

The dawn came up and dim light filtered down through the tall pines. The Schulzes had left me an hour previously. I had asked about the diversion. Hans Schulz said, "You will hear. When you hear – "

"What will I hear? Firing, or the grenades?"

"Firing first. That will be the signal that the crossing is about to be made. You will descend as fast as you can to the east, towards the border wire." In fact we had been coming down for the last half-hour and Schulz had said that the dawn would show me that I was not far from the wire, a matter of a thousand yards or so, where it ran through the forest. I'd asked him earlier, in his house, how the crossing would be made and he said he hadn't been told – it was always, he rightly said, a case of the right hand being better off in ignorance of what the left hand was doing. Such was virtually the theme song of my own life as an agent of 6D2. As I waited interminably, as that dawn came and proved Schulz right in that I could see the border ahead of me and a little below, and seeming in some disarray on account of the repair work, I thought about the various ways that had been tried, the different attempts, some successful, others not, to cross from the East into freedom. Many of them had been in the area of the Berlin Wall: straight and foolish attempts to run like a rabbit from the guns only to be colandered and left to twitch to death; suicidal dashes in heavy vehicles; persons concealed in car boots at the Corridor check-points, or in crates aboard lorries; tunnelling, helicopters, grappling irons and ropes. Crop-spraying aircraft had been used with success, a mass escape years ago had been made aboard a train that had crashed through the barriers; a fire-engine had achieved a similar success. It still remained – I would have thought – virtually impossible to get through the electrified fences, through the minefields, past the watch-towers, one of which I could see now, over the trip-wires and away from the shrapnel-firing booby traps. But it had been done. That was hard fact, no argument. The mind and body of your oppressed seeker of freedom can achieve miracles.

Half frozen now by inactivity, the over-riding need not at this juncture to draw attention by any movement, I went on watching through my binoculars and listening out for Schulz' diversion, watching for some sight of the woman who would presumably not show until the last possible moment. The trees had been cleared for some distance on both sides of the defences, which contained more than one layer of wire, and what looked like a bit of a gap right through, with temporary barriers. The actual border was marked with an upstanding post, painted red, yellow and black in diagonal stripes, and there was a sign which I was able to read through my binoculars:

24

ACHTUNG!
BACHMITTE
GRENZE

the first and third words being in black, the BACHMITTE in
red. Just to the left of the border post, beyond no-man's-
land and on the other side of the wire, was a grey watch-
tower. There would be no cover from the remaining trees,
no help there until the open ground had been traversed.
The attempt looked like madness, bound to fail. But
Schulz had seemed confident.

Then I heard the shooting.

Just a single shot to begin with; then a fusillade of sub-
machine gun fire. Away to the north, through the trees as
I started my downhill scramble towards the frontier, I
caught a brief glimpse of the Schulzes, all three of them,
weaving their guns in a wide swathe, then they retreated
into cover, all except one of the sons who remained in full
view for a moment longer as he flung a succession of
grenades towards armed soldiers running out from the East
German watch-tower. As the return fire started up the
young Schulz vanished suddenly: I didn't know whether
or not he had been hit. I went on blindly down the
slope, feeling the pumping of my heart. Then the miracle
happened: ahead of me, running like the wind itself on the
far side of the border, a slim figure in tattered clothing
appeared behind a series of small explosions that I took,
rightly, to be land mines going off – the woman was
coming on behind a herd of deer, unwitting sacrifices to
touch off the mines, and I saw the pathetic animals lying
shattered in writhing hummocks as the ground erupted
beyond the wire, beyond the temporarily filled gap in the
defences. Then the human figure vanished for a moment
until I picked it up again, close to the barrier and climbing.

Schulz had been right: no electrification.

My heart thumped.

But now troops were coming along fast from the watch-
tower, making for the woman. As they ran, the Schulzes

came back into the action, pumping away with the sub-machine guns, not I thought to kill but to keep the East Germans back as far as possible. The East Germans hesitated and the climbing figure threw itself from the barrier and started squirming on its stomach across no-man's-land towards the security of the West as the Schulzes kept up their fire and held the guards off.

She seemed to be making it: miracle was the word – I couldn't believe my eyes really, couldn't believe the clumsiness of the attempt, couldn't believe she had got as far as she had and never mind the element of luck that had been so strongly in her favour.

But the miracle didn't last.

As the squirming figure came on the East Germans at last reacted in gunfire. Bullets swathed across, a sustained racket in the sharp cold. The woman reared up, screaming, fell back again, dragged herself on a few more feet until she lifted again, slewed, fell back, rolled over and lay still. As she did so the point of aim of the East German guards shifted and the guns fired in wide sweeps towards where I'd last seen the Schulzes. I didn't see them again and I couldn't say if they had been hit. By this time the military West was reacting as well: from the north what looked like British tracked vehicles were moving in and as they closed I heard a lot of barneying through loudhailers on both sides. It was going to be a military and diplomatic nightmare from now on and one I would personally be obliged to avoid. But I knew it was my duty, not that of the British troops, to approach that dissident and make quite sure she was dead; she just might not be, she just might be able to speak, she might even – though this was unlikely to say the least – have something documentary. And she had come a long way, and through unbelievable danger, to contact someone from the West.

So far, under the eyes and no doubt the guns of the British Army of the Rhine, the East Germans were not sticking out their necks by coming over the frontier to pull the woman back behind the Curtain. But it was only a few seconds after this that I saw why: as once again the snow began falling thickly and the visibility came right down I saw the lick of flame, small at first and then quickly becoming a roar, a jet like a blow-torch: the bastards were using a flame-thrower. It came through the snowfall like a fiery sword, licked along the body, which again reared up and writhed and began to crisp, catching fire so that small blue flames danced and she became a husk.

I was sick on the ground. Literally. It was a terrible sight. And it had been a doomed attempt from the start, one that should never have been attempted and of course wouldn't have been if 6D2, or even M16 who gather overseas intelligence under the aegis of the Foreign Office, had been in charge throughout rather than have left it to the Ladybirds. As Arthur Webb had said. I wasn't impressed, I have to say, by the Ladybirds at that stage: one can play things too close to the chest sometimes.

I beat retreat, feeling very bad about it all, with the snowfall worsening fast. The job was over before it had started – but that, I knew, was a simplification. It wouldn't be back to Focal House for Miss Mandrake and me. Max would regard the assignment as continuing, only just begun rather than ended. The information that hadn't got through was said to be vital: I would have to dig on my own now, set up a network and start the probe. And I had nothing to go on beyond one dead girl, name unknown, and a hornet's nest about to break upon the world via the press, the sort of thing 6D2 always does its best to avoid. Max wasn't going to be pleased.

I headed back on a mental compass bearing for the cover of the virgin forest, and when I hit the trees, which I almost did literally, so thick was that blinding snow, I tried to pick up the track for Braunlage. It would have been useless to make any attempt to locate the Schulzes. If they'd got away, then I'd make contact with them at their home in the forest. It was quite a climb back, with my sense of direction all haywire in the snow-storm, and then a long descent down the other side, pushing through the pines and the undergrowth. When I came down to more or less level ground I found I was well south of Braunlage and I was faced with a long walk to the Schulz home. By the time I got there, it was nine hours since I'd left, before that day's dawn. Now it was past 1300 hours and the snow was falling still, which as I realized later was why there were no footprints or other marks visible. When I knocked politely at the front door there was no answer, and after another knock I turned the handle and went in.

The house was silent, and very cold.

I went into the sitting-room where we'd drunk lager the night before. The fire was almost out, just a few embers and a woody smell. No-one there: I went upstairs, taking them two at a time, really worried now. The first bedroom I came to was that of Hans and his wife. I opened the door unceremoniously. Frau Schulz lay on the bed, her face seeming more granite than ever in death. The head lolled sideways as though it had little contact with the body, which indeed was the case: the throat had been cut and there was a good deal of blood everywhere. I left the room and ran to what had been Felicity's room. It was empty and there were signs of a struggle, the bedclothes all over the show, a chair overturned, all Felicity's things from the dressing-table scattered on the floor, and a streak of blood, dried blood, on the dressing-table itself.

Knowing it was useless, I searched the house from top to bottom. Nothing, no clues, no other signs of alarm, struggle or disturbance. What remained was the hard fact that someone had got hold of Felicity. I didn't doubt that she was still alive. And my mind settled into a twin groove, the obvious one as it seemed to me: the KGB or their East German agents, or Greenfly.

I went back into the deserted sitting-room. Half a minute later the telephone rang.

3

The instrument was in the hall: I went out and I looked at it, letting it ring and trying to make up my mind, which was a shade disorientated for the moment. Did I answer or did I not? The first thing, really, was to make contact with our London HQ, or maybe the Bonn one who would have been put in the picture initially by Focal House. With no real reason I had a hunch the caller would be connected with recent events: in point of fact it could be anyone, a friend of the Schulzes asking them out for a meal, a girl ringing one of the sons. But my hunch said it wasn't anything so innocent. I could have been watched, the house could have been watched and my return noted. If I didn't answer – what then?

Two things: the caller would come in person, or, and I believed more likely, he would know I was there and wasn't answering, that I was following my suspicions, that he might thereby be in danger and he would scarper for the time being.

I picked up the receiver and said in not very good German, "Hullo."

A voice, a man's voice, said, "Commander Shaw."

"You sound very certain. Do I know you?" I couldn't identify the voice, but I didn't think it was German, and it certainly wasn't English.

"We have met, yes. We should meet again. In your own interest, Commander Shaw."

I asked him who he was. All he said was, "You must

trust me. You come, or you do not come. I cannot force this. It is up to you."

"Too right, it is," I said coolly. "If you want to meet me, I suggest you come here and – "

"No. We shall meet elsewhere. A little to the west of Bad Harzburg is a ski lodge. Driving out ten miles from Bad Harzburg it is on the left of the road and cannot be missed. The Three Kings . . . I shall wait in the car park. You will park and I shall come."

The call was cut. He hadn't even asked for particulars of my car, from which it could be assumed he knew already, unless he had known me so well in the past that he would recognise me when I got out. Very likely he did and would, but I was quite unable to place him from the voice and usually I'm hot on voices; they're almost impossible to disguise if you're not a professional actor, there's always a give-away to the alert ear. My caller hadn't stipulated a time, which meant soonest possible, and, having made up my mind, I didn't delay. The juxtaposition of events told me that the man might have information about Felicity, and if so there was urgency so far as I was concerned. It wasn't surprising that Max disliked intimacy and involvement, emotional involvement, on the part of his field force: I would lean over backwards where danger to Felicity was concerned. We were everything short of married: we both preferred her to remain Miss Mandrake while we were still at 6D2's beck and call for world wide assignments; one day I would retire, and then so would she, willy nilly, but that day was a long way off yet. We both liked the spice of danger and the cash was good, very good. It would continue until the shakes set in in my hands and I had built up a large enough private income to survive inflation. But in the meantime Felicity brought her anxieties and I couldn't wait to get on the track.

I had a good road map of the Continent and I was on my way to Bad Harzburg within five minutes of the telephone

30

call. The Schulzes hadn't turned up and I couldn't afford to wait. The fact of their continuing absence meant, probably, that they'd all died under the East German guns, and I was desperately sorry it had, or might have, turned out that way for them all; but it was a risk that everyone remotely connected with 6D2 faced all the time and they'd have known that risk. They'd felt it worth while, either for the political aspect or the cash, or both. My talk with Hans Schulz the night before had told me he and his family detested communism and the Hitler-like threat it posed so close physically to their own lives, and I believed their mainspring was simple patriotism, a nice old-fashioned concept.

It was a nasty drive in the snow, though the fall had thinned by now and the traffic was keeping the roads open. There was filthy slush and a strong tendency to skid had to be controlled. I passed through Bad Harzburg and continued west until I saw groups of skiers on both sides of the road, some of them crossing towards what looked like the ski lodge and was.

I pulled into the car park, moving slow between the groups of men and women carrying skis and ski sticks, all colourfully dressed, all carefree and happy, not having any rendezvous with international thuggery and duplicity. I wished them all the luck in the world in getting away from what, in the majority of cases anyway, their working lives would be like: offices, accounts, sales, the rat race and the arrogance of those who'd made it over them. That would never have been for me. I got out and looked around. Opposite the main building there was a ski shop, with plenty of comings and goings. Near the ski shop was a big Volvo with a man behind the wheel, a man dressed in black and wearing a black homburg hat. He had a waiting look; his fingers drummed on the steering wheel and he kept glancing into his mirrors. In the back of the Volvo two more men sat, wearing anoraks. I was beginning to recognise the man in black: there was no doubt that we

31

had met before but I've met hundreds of men and women, good and bad, and it didn't click straight off.

But he was my man, all right.

I approached the car. I had my revolver in a shoulder holster, though I didn't expect anything like a shoot-out in so public a place. As I went up to the driving window the man turned to face me and then I knew. I said, "Storvac. Bosko Storvac! I thought you were dead."

The face was bleak and pale. It split into a brief smile. "So did many people, but you see I am not."

My mind, as I stood there beside the Volvo, went back into a distant past. There had been a bomb and I and several others had been convinced Storvac had been in the middle of the explosion. Storvac, a Yugoslav, had been, presumably still was, a member of WUSWIPP. So I hadn't been off the track when I'd seen a WUSWIPP connection with my flat and the squat, crudely-drawn greenfly.

I asked, "What do you want, Storvac?"

He said, "Please get into the car." He reached across to open the front passenger door but I told him to wait a minute.

"I'm getting into no car," I said. "Not with you, Storvac."

"You wish to know . . . what I have to tell you. You wish to know about Miss Mandrake."

I felt my heart miss a beat. Of course I wanted to know. But I said, "Not alone with you and your tame thugs in the back. If you don't get out for a private talk, Storvac, I'll simply drive away. You won't stop me. You won't start anything here."

Storvac shrugged. "You would drive away along roads that in many places are quiet, where shooting can take place. But I wish you no harm, Commander Shaw. Had I wished this, then I would have suggested a more private place of meeting, no?"

"Probably no," I said sarcastically. "I might not have come, might I?"

32

"You are being obstinate."

"Absolutely – dead right. If you're on the level, prove it. Get out and come into the restaurant. I'll buy you a coffee. Not your bully boys. Just you, Storvac. In there, we're both of us safe from the other." I paused. "Aren't you sticking your neck out, Storvac? Or aren't you wanted, in West Germany?"

The pale face smiled again, as briefly as before. "No."

"It must be the only place outside the Curtain where you're not."

"Perhaps so. But I am not to be swayed by compliments."

"Nor me by sick jokes. Leave the car, or bugger off."

"Very well, I shall go," he said angrily, and switched the ignition on. He started to back out of his parking space, eyes ahead and using his mirrors. He was watching me at the same time, waiting for me to be overcome by curiosity and concern for Felicity, and weaken. I wasn't going to. I fancied I had Storvac's measure and had had it for a long time over the earlier years. Storvac, who was a WUSWIPP backroom boy, a pure scientist rather than a strong-arm, was short on endurance. His sticking point was fairly low, or had been. It still was. He circled the car park, narrowly missing the crowds as they stamped through the snow, and came back to where I was waiting.

"Very well," he said snappishly. "For now I do as you wish." He got out, leaned back in for a word with his gunmen, a word I didn't catch, then straightened and banged the door. We crunched away and went up some ice-covered steps to the restaurant foyer, where a number of skiers were clustered around a big relief map of the area showing the ski runs and so on. The place was pretty crowded but we found a table for two in a corner by a window where we could talk in relative privacy – there was a loud buzz of conversation interspersed with hearty laughter, the latter coming from a bunch of British hooray henries who might have been Oxbridge undergraduates or

33

Guards' subalterns. Inane, but I was glad just then of their lack of inhibition.

A girl came up smiling and I ordered coffee and biscuits. It was all rather incongruous; as innocent as a hen party in Harrods in the middle of a tiring shopping morning – on the surface. While we waited for the girl to come back, I said, "Right, Storvac. You can start now."

"Very well. I start with your flat in London."

"So you do know about that."

"Yes."

"Who was responsible?"

"WUSWIPP."

"I thought as much. You, Storvac?" I was pretty sure it wouldn't have been: not Storvac's style.

"Not me. Greenfly."

"Ah yes, Greenfly. I think you'd better explain about Greenfly, Storvac. Where does he, or she, or it come in?"

"Greenfly is an it. A grouping within WUSWIPP – "

"A new one on me, Storvac. What are they after?"

"Information."

"Which is why they ransacked my flat. They might have known, they might have credited me with a better awareness of security than that – don't you think, Storvac?"

To my surprise he agreed. "Greenfly are inexperienced, they are young tearaways as you would say, a thorn in the flesh of WUSWIPP. They wish to move too fast, sometimes too far as well."

I nodded. "I've been hearing rumours, not about Greenfly but about WUSWIPP . . . I've not come up against WUSWIPP personally for some time now. I'm told you're moderating your views and aspirations, that you're learning sense, learning at last what you're likely to project the world into. Am I right?"

"Yes," Storvac said. "At any rate, you come close. There has been a shift – the world is becoming too dangerous a place as between East and West, and – "

"Thanks largely to WUSWIPP."

"I say again there has been a shift – "

"And the Greenfly faction are reactionaries?"

"Yes," he said.

The girl came with the coffee and biscuits. A pot and two cups – I poured, and politely passed the plate of biscuits. Storvac's hand hovered and then came down on a chocolate one. I saw for the first time that he had two false hands, very well constructed but too perfect, working on a system that I'd heard about, impulses and reflexes and so on. Looking at them I asked, "That bomb?"

He nodded. He hadn't got away totally unscathed, but it was a miracle he'd lived at all. I suspected further damage – his voice was higher than it had once been, which was why I hadn't picked it up on the telephone in the Schulz house. Using restraint I didn't ask embarrassing questions: no point in antagonising someone who might – just might – be, however oddly, on our side. I said, "All right, Storvac. Go on. Let's come to Miss Mandrake. Where is she, and who's got her?"

"Greenfly," he said. "In East Germany. For now."

"You mean she's going farther east?"

"Yes."

"Why?"

"A hostage," he said, as I'd expected. "And for any information she might have."

"She hasn't. And information about *what*, for God's sake?"

Storvac smiled that icy smile, a short summer briefly superimposed upon bleak mid-winter. "Since you do not know what about, you cannot be sure Miss Mandrake hasn't got it!"

I said, "Oh yes, I can. She knows nothing that I don't, Storvac."

"If you say so, Commander Shaw. But this, Greenfly will not know, and they will probe."

"Torture," I said flatly.

"Yes, regrettably."

35

"Can't you," I said with heat and bitterness, "control your lunatic fringe, Storvac?"

"No," he said. "The bit between the tooth. Now, Commander." He leaned across the table, his face close to mine. His breath smelled stale, betraying stomach trouble. Quickly I lit a cigarette. "Greenfly have got hold of something which we, the main body of WUSWIPP, do not know about. But we believe it to be lethal knowledge, lethal for peace – "

"You used not to worry about peace, Storvac, and never mind what WUSWIPP officially stood for."

"Did you not listen when I said that things have changed? There are so many developments – weapons in space, missiles and anti-missile missiles, lasers, germ warfare. Star wars policies. Both sides are as bad – "

"But WUSWIPP has always been firmly in the Soviet camp, Storvac."

"Yes. We still are. I am taking a risk in meeting with you here. Or anywhere. You see, we in WUSWIPP wish to restrain the Soviet leadership by wise counsel – "

"What a hope!"

"No. Some of them understand only too well, but they find their voices silenced by the military, who are effectively in charge of policy behind the scenes." Storvac waved an arm. "You may say, Commander Shaw, that it has been our own scientific research and development that has provided the military with its weapons of mass destruction. You are right. But it has overtaken itself now and there is a time to call a halt."

"But Greenfly doesn't agree. Haven't you any ideas what it is they've got hold of?"

Storvac shook his head. He met my eyes. He said, "No, we have not." I believed he was sincere; I asked him what he imagined I or 6D2 or even the British Government could do about something happening in Russia that wasn't known even to the flapping ears and prodding noses of WUSWIPP. He said, "I cannot say. Perhaps nothing. But

36

you have become involved now, Commander Shaw. You were here to meet the woman. That means your people are taking an interest."

"The woman," I said. "Who was she? Not that it's important. She was just a messenger. But what do you know of the Ladybirds, Storvac?"

He shrugged. "Mere dissidents."

"They seem to know more than you or your WUSWIPP comrades."

"Yes."

"So why don't you direct your efforts towards the Ladybirds? Or have you done just that – without success?"

"Yes," he said again. "They are dedicated. They refuse to speak, either to us or to the KGB. Some have gone to mental institutions. Some have gone to Siberia. Many have died."

"More torture," I said, and thought about Felicity. I looked beyond Storvac, out through the window. The sun was shining now but it was late in the day and soon the dusk would come, and then perhaps more snow. The Harz region was beautiful, impressive, but the approach of night once again gave it menace and foreboding, it became again the kind of region where anything could happen. I wondered where Felicity was: it wouldn't have been diffi-cult to smuggle her across the border, at any rate with East German connivance. I cursed myself for not having contacted the army authorities, say at Minden, and reported her missing. I'd been in too much of a hurry to follow up Storvac's telephone call . . . and anyway Max wouldn't have thanked me for bringing in the military in the middle of an undercover assignment. 6D2 doesn't work that way. Agents are out on a limb, always, and don't run for help. Once in the field, they are no longer recognised. But I thought, now, that I'd owed it to Felicity to go against Max for once. Too late, however.

Storvac was speaking again. "You have come here to

37

West Germany to find out the same information as I. Why should we not work together?"

"Why should I trust you, Storvac?"

"Because you have no option, I think. And time, for all we know, may be short." He paused. "This much we know – that there has been much coming and going at the Defence Ministry in Moscow for some days past, with high-ranking officers and Party members attending."

"So? Is that unusual?"

Storvac said, "This time we believe it may be significant."

I paid for the coffee and biscuits and left the restaurant with Storvac. For good or ill I had made my decision: I was putting myself in his hands. It was the only way I saw of carrying out my assignment, of making contact with the Ladybirds, the eaters of greenflies, and of following up the only lead I had to Felicity Mandrake. Storvac was insistent that something was brewing inside the Soviet Union, that matters were coming to a head and that Greenfly was deeply involved. All that, of course, accorded with what Arthur Webb had told me only yesterday in Focal House. To get at any information, now that the border crossing had ended in failure, I had to put myself the other side of the Iron Curtain. Storvac didn't foresee any difficulties so long as I travelled with him. His WUSWIPP papers would see his car through all the check points on the Corridor. With those papers, as an Eastern Bloc VIP, there would positively be no East German boot inspection at Checkpoint Charlie, and I wouldn't, he said, need to be in discomfort for long.

We left the car park in the two cars, Storvac's Volvo following my Volkswagen. The light was going now and the temperature was already dropping; the roads would be tricky as the slushy snow began to freeze. Some distance beyond the ski lodge, Storvac had said, there was a lay-by half way down a steep and winding hill where my car

38

could in the prevailing weather conditions be convincingly disposed of. That, he said, and I agreed, would be the best. Afterwards, people could read into it what they wished but there would be no proof of anything one way or the other.

We took the first part of the journey fairly fast. My headlamps picked out the lay-by round a bend, a wide space with a wooden fence. Beyond, Storvac had said, was a long drop, with thickly-growing pines on the other side. He had also said there wouldn't be much traffic around and he was right: we had scarcely passed a single car. As I approached, I threw the Volkswagen into a skid that churned up the snow nicely, and stopped some yards short of the fence. Behind me, Storvac slowed. I put the car in neutral, headed it for the far end of the fence, released the handbrake, got out into the snow, and pushed hard. The Volkswagen gathered speed down the slope of the lay-by and crashed through the fence, hurtled down that long drop and, as an added bonus, caught fire. I saw the flames, small at first then shooting up into the trees. Storvac came up as I began scuffing the snow about to obliterate my footprints, though with any luck more snow would soon come to do its own work on them. This done, I got into the front passenger seat of the Volvo and with no more time lost Storvac headed away north to slot himself into the Corridor for Berlin.

I wondered how long it would be before the wreckage was found and how long it would be before Max in Focal House, hearing that I was now out of contact and that the Ladybird had failed to get through, would start putting two and two together and getting it wrong.

It was a lonely feeling.

You can't deviate from the Corridor. It was Berlin or nothing. I'd known all along that Storvac's concept of 'not long' in the boot wasn't mine. By the time I was released I was more than boot weary; I was cramped into immobility and we were safely through Checkpoint Charlie and right out of the eastern sector of Berlin. I didn't need Storvac to tell me that even for non-VIPs Checkpoint Charlie presented few problems nowadays when going from west to east – it would have been a different matter the other way round, but these days plenty of tourists went through and things were more relaxed than a few years ago. Now we were heading for Russia via Poland – Poznan, Warsaw, Minsk in the Byelorussian Socialist Soviet Republic – a long drive, something over 700 miles from Berlin, and then perhaps some more since Minsk wouldn't be journey's end – or not necessarily. It seemed Storvac had a handy stopover there. I could use it as a base of operations if I wished.

I said, "It might be as good as anywhere."

I thought about the huge vastness of the Russian land mass and had to admit to myself that I hadn't any notion of where to begin. Or how. Felicity could be anywhere. The one hope was that WUSWIPP would have some information as to the whereabouts of its Greenfly faction – and even they would presumably be pretty widespread. Indeed, Storvac had already said as much. After Berlin he had handed over the driving to one of his thugs, a taciturn Russian who didn't appear to have much if any English and sat glaring through the windscreen like an angry bear and gripping the wheel as though his life depended on it. Talk about tension, I thought – and the tension, as we penetrated deeper into Poland, had gripped me as well. This was the land of Walesa, of oppression of trade unions, of priestly murder, of the sudden visit in the dead of night, and somehow it managed to feel like it. I had been behind the Curtain before now, many times, but never quite like this, in a WUSWIPP car and not knowing what the next step might be. I looked out at a wintry landscape, snow as far as the eye could see, and at bleak industrial complexes as we came through or past towns, towers and chimneys rising into an iron-hard sky. Storvac seemed happier than he'd been in West Germany – after all, he was homeward bound and already in friendly territory. Even though he hadn't been a wanted man in West Germany, he must have felt uneasy. We chatted; he wasn't an unfriendly man. I remembered that he had been married. I asked about his wife. She had died two years ago and he had been very lonely. He had immersed himself in his work for WUSWIPP and the Party. He had, he said, two children, a boy and a girl, both now married and living far from his home, so he didn't see much of them. He sounded sad; it may have been his sadness at that moment that struck me as particularly un-WUSWIPP-like: I'd never associated that bunch of bastards with domesticity or love of children, even their own children. But now, it seemed, they'd at last begun to be sickened by their own rottenness, by all they'd done in the past to make the world potentially a more dangerous, a more lethal place if war should come.

Minsk is situated in old White Russia; the area around is fairly open country, traversed by hills that form the watershed between the Baltic and Black Sea basins, though part of it is flatter and well wooded, with extensive marshes. Minsk itself, Storvac told me, had a flourishing industry – cars and commercial vehicles, machine tools, radio and TV equipment, foodstuffs, pharmaceuticals, general consumer goods. There had been growth in recent years and there had been a lot of new building. As we drove into the outskirts I saw this new building for myself: it was grim and characterless, row upon row of workers' dwellings, high-rise flats for the most part, and barrack-like factories, and a dead cold wind blowing and bringing snow, a heavy fall that started just as we approached the city, and began to settle on the buildings so that by the time we had reached Storvac's stopover a good deal of the ugliness had been overlaid.

Storvac's driver pulled the Volvo into the side of a street of warehouses and Storvac got out, motioning me to follow.

There were not many people around – it was evening now and the weather was no doubt keeping the Russian workers indoors – but such as there were stared curiously at the expensive car and its obviously well-fed occupants. Foreign cars were uncommon inside Russia to say the least, and the faces of the onlookers showed envy and a degree of hostility, not too overt in case the occupants should be KGB. As we moved away Storvac said, "We are conspicuous, you see."

"So you don't take the Volvo all the way?"

"That is so, yes." We walked on, crunching over snow frozen from an earlier fall, coat collars pulled up against the fresh blizzard; it wasn't far short of that. We left the main thoroughfare and turned off to the left, past two more turnings, then left again, then right. Ahead I saw a tall block of flats, with lights coming on behind thin curtains. Storvac made for this. I followed behind him into a sort of lobby, a square place of bare and dirty concrete covered with graffiti as to the walls, with what appeared to be a depiction of President Reagan ahead of a monstrous penis rudely aimed – to the charitable it could have been a missile but I wasn't feeling charitable. Storvac led the way up a flight of concrete stairs: there were two lifts, but both were out of action. "Vandalised," Storvac said.

"So you have them too."

"Yes. The discipline is not good now. Not what it was, as regards the young, though Gorbachev does what he can."

"Sad," I said, tongue in cheek. Storvac turned and gave me a dirty look.

"You in the West," he said, "are worse. Strikes, always strikes. And everyone taking drugs. And the police being viciously against the workers."

I shrugged; there was no point in arguing, in making comparisons with the KGB for instance. From now on, for the foreseeable future, Storvac was a mate. So I followed my old mate up seven storeys and there he stopped at a scuffed door and banged twice. There was no answer and he gave the door a push, a shake and a rattle. It didn't seem to be bolted, just held on something like a Yale lock, not all that secure.

"Yasnov must be out," he said. "That is tiresome."

"So what do we do, Storvac?"

He seemed uncertain and much put out. He dithered; and as he dithered I heard something. It was a low groan; low as it was, it carried an immensity of pain. I said, "Yasnov could be out, I suppose. But someone isn't."

4

At Storvac's request I put my shoulder to the door and butted hard. The lock broke away and the door flew open and we crashed in. We heard the groans again, coming from a room opening off to the right of a narrow hallway, and we went in fast. Never had I seen anything like the scene: I was confronted by a rough cross screwed into a wall, a cross with the naked body of a young woman hanging from it with blood coming from the outstretched hands and from the crossed ankles. It took me several seconds before I realized I was watching a crucifixion, even though I knew crucifixion had by no means died out with the diabolical earthly death of Jesus of Nazareth. They still make use of it today in some of the Middle Eastern countries and there is quite a sale for crucifixion equipment. I had read somewhere about the process and until I'd read it I'd simply had no idea, no possible conception of what a terrible death crucifixion is. The nails themselves, driven through some particularly agonising nerve, bring ceaseless pain; but death occurs by strangulation, oddly enough to the layman. Not so much strangulation as suffocation: the way the body's weight falls lifts up the lungs or diaphragm so that breathing becomes almost impossible. In the early pre-Christian days, nails were not in fact driven through the ankles: the body hung directly from the hands so that the suffocation process was faster; then some bright bastard dreamed up the nailed-ankle idea. A real brainwave; with the weight to that extent taken off, the agony of dying lasted much longer.

All this passed through my mind as Storvac and I went into action. The idea, I said, was first to lay the body flat so that its weight came off; and we were tugging at the cross when some of the retaining screws gave way too suddenly, pulling out from the wall behind, and cross and body crashed down on us, spattering us with blood. We struggled clear, turned the cross over so that the body was laid on its back, and Storvac went on a hunt for something with which to pull out nails. And now I saw that in falling the girl had struck her head on a metal bracket looking as though it had once held a washbasin. The metal had penetrated the skull and had broken the bone away as the body had gone on down. There was a lot of mess and the girl was out of her misery.

I got to my feet as Storvac came back, having found no handy implement. I said, "Too late, Storvac."

"She is dead?"

"Yes, very. Do you know who she was?"

He said, "Yasnov's daughter Irina." Storvac was trembling and his face was paler than ever, all blood seeming to have left it. "She was nineteen years of age. Just nineteen years, Commander."

As he finished speaking there was a sound in the hallway, footsteps coming in from the open front door. I reached for my shoulder holster but as a man entered Storvac put a restraining hand on my arm. I saw the reactions in the man's face: a welcome for Storvac, some alarm at the sight of me, a stranger, then the shock and horror as he saw what lay on the floor. Like Storvac, he shook. He knelt down by the body. Storvac went to him and put an arm about his shoulder.

"What can I say, Igor, my friend?"

"Who did this?" Tears were streaming, the face was haunted.

"I do not know. We found her – "

"I have been out all day at work and she was alone, my little daughter who is all I had left."

No mention of a wife: I assumed the man was a widower. He got to his feet, staggering, his face buried now in his hands. I left the room and went out into the hall, then into another room where there was a scrubbed wooden table and chairs, and a sink and a dresser. I opened cupboard doors in the dresser and found what I was looking for, a bottle of vodka. I took this, with a glass, to the room where Irina Yasnov lay, caught Yasnov's eye, lifted my eyebrows at him and began to pour. He snatched the bottle from my hand and put the neck to his mouth, and tilted it. Then, when he had taken what he needed, he looked at me and addressed me for the first time. In Russian, asking me, I was able to understand, who I was. I lifted a restraining hand and said in a whisper to Storvac, "Say to him – not so fast. We'll go on a bug hunt first."

"Bugs, yes." Storvac whispered in Yasnov's ear and then we had a good look round and it wasn't wasted time: I found two small devices in the flat, one in the kitchen-cum-living room, one in the bedroom where the body lay, and I ripped them out. I carried on the search but didn't find any more. As an added precaution I switched on a battery radio that I'd found in the kitchen: the damn thing didn't work.

"We'll keep our voices low," I said, "just in case. So in a whisper, Storvac, you can confide in Yasnov."

He did so. "A British agent," Yasnov said softly, glaring at me.

"But friendly, Igor. You have my assurance. He is not here to act against the Soviet. Only against Greenfly, like you and I."

Yasnov took another pull at the bottle. "It is Greenfly who has done this. I know it." He paced the room, passing and repassing the broken, crucified body, his face working. I had understood his Russian and I fancied he could be right, although I would have expected to find the green bug emblem, as in my own flat. There seemed to be no love lost between the old guard of WUSWIPP and

46

Greenfly. After a few more pacings Yasnov halted and swung round on me, and spoke in just understandable English.

"What do you know of Greenfly, Englishman?"

I said, "Nothing, Comrade Yasnov. I'm here to find out. I hope you'll help me."

There was a grunt and then Yasnov and Storvac began speaking Russian and I was largely lost. While they were talking I heard the bang at the front door and then footsteps in the hall and the two men, the two thugs from the Volvo, came in. One of them reported to Storvac, something about the car – Storvac told me later that they had garaged it in a warehouse managed by a friend. Then the new arrivals saw the body, or rather the sheet that by this time Storvac had placed over it. There was much natural consternation and the KGB was mentioned; presumably the murder would have to be reported to some authority or other but I hoped it wasn't to be the KGB. So, I gathered, did Storvac. The involvement of the KGB would complicate matters for more than just me. There was a personal element in all this, the vendetta between WUSWIPP and the break-away killers of Greenfly, and Storvac didn't want any State interference at this stage. There was a good deal of argument, Igor Yasnov grew a little drunk on vodka, and passed the bottle round. It was soon empty. Irina Yasnova still lay on the floor beneath the sheet while her disposal was discussed: I found that gruesome, and left the room, going back again to the kitchen where I'd found the vodka. I flicked off the light and circumspectly peered from behind the curtain. The snow was falling heavily, obscuringly, and no-one was about. It was a whitened scene of total and brooding silence. Somewhere in this vast country was Felicity. I saw her in my mind's eye, lying like Irina Yasnova, crucified, tortured by inhuman hands, the antennae of Greenfly. But I was being too fanciful: a hostage wouldn't be killed. Not so soon, anyway. But I

47

might need to be fast, and to date I had got nowhere, and time was passing too quickly.

As I came away from that high-up window, thinking my unproductive thoughts, Storvac joined me. Checking the curtain, he switched on the light. He said, "We have been discussing the body."

"I got that far," I said. "Any decisions yet?"

"Igor Yasnov is friendly with a person who was formerly a People's Judge for the constituency. He will be asked for advice and help."

"He won't stick his neck out against the KGB, Storvac. Or will he?"

"Yasnov says he is a good friend, and was fond of Irina and of her mother."

"Who is dead?"

Storvac nodded. "Yes, dead."

The way he said it made me ask how she had died. He said, "She was raped to death, Commander, by men of the KGB, drunken men. And I repeat, this friend of Yasnov's was fond of her and would have married her if Igor Yasnov had not done so."

"I see," I said. I went on, "I've been wondering, how was Irina crucified . . . without anyone overhearing, without anyone interfering? I assume all these flats are occupied?"

"Only sparsely during the day," Storvac answered. "In Russia everyone works, or almost everyone other than the old. As to interfering . . ." He shrugged. "You are a man of the world, after all."

"Yes," I said. Inside Russia, anywhere behind the Iron Curtain, also in certain states of South America and elsewhere, the prudent never interfere. You just let screams happen and you cover your ears if you're squeamish. All the same, I'd have thought sheer curiosity alone would have brought doors ajar and faces peering from behind curtains as the killers left. But then I remembered what Storvac had just said about the KGB rape. There would be people here who would recall that, people who knew that sometimes screams were due to the KGB, people who would be taking no chances thereafter; and I accepted Storvac's point.

I said, "This People's Judge. Are you going to tell him about me?"

Storvac said, "He might be of help to you."

"It's a risk. I can't say I'm keen."

"You will not get far in Russia without help."

"I have your promise of yours, Storvac. I believe that's good enough."

"It is for you to decide. I shall do as you wish."

"Then keep quiet about me to anyone close to officialdom."

"Very well. What do you propose to do now?"

"Start looking for Miss Mandrake," I said, "and she'll lead me to Greenfly. I know it's a needle in a haystack, you needn't remind me. But one thing has a habit of leading to another, right?"

"Perhaps," Storvac agreed, and then gave a ghost of a smile. "But so far, I think, you have not got the one thing."

"Never mind," I said, and then added, "But perhaps I have, if we're assuming it was Greenfly that killed Irina Yasnov."

"How so?"

"The dog to its vomit. They'll be around somewhere, just to see what the reaction is."

Storvac didn't offer any comment on that. He left me again, going back to the others in the crucifixion room, and a few minutes later he left the flat with Yasnov, making, I assumed, for this People's Judge. I was left with the two strong-arm boys from the Volvo, taciturn men and watchful. I could see the bulges of the shoulder holsters and even though they knew I was a mate of Storvac's, those bulges had to be reckoned with. Do anything they didn't like and they would react. Not that I could do

49

anything but wait for Storvac's return. I tried to be friendly in the meantime, smiling at them and trying some Russian, but they didn't respond. After I'd uttered a few platitudinous sentences one of them came up with some brief colloquial English.

"Shut up," he said.

Storvac and Yasnov were absent a little over two hours, the longest two hours of my life to date. I was having nightmares about Greenfly watching and seeing me when I emerged, and possibly recognising me. Storvac had mentioned some names of the known break-away group and although they hadn't rung any bells with me I knew there would be others, the ones whose names even Storvac didn't know, whom I could have come up against in the past. And when they recognised me they would probably lose no time in making a report to the KGB if only to discredit Storvac and Yasnov and the official WUSWIPP. It wouldn't do WUSWIPP any good at all to be tarred with the brush of collaboration with a Western agent and all would naturally be grist to Greenfly's mill. I had been helpful to the Soviet government in the past but that was purely in the interest of a specific job, the time I'd been called upon to stop Rollerball in its tracks before its huge explosive power shattered the world's peace, and on that occasion I'd entered the Soviet Union by invitation and was thus well sponsored. Not so this time; I'd come in as a straight-out undercover man, a spy, if with the best of intentions and no enmity towards the Soviet . . .

Storvac and Yasnov came back. Storvac said, "It has been decided. The body is to be disposed of."

I asked, "When and how?"

"Tonight. Irina will be driven out of Minsk, to the marshlands. Afterwards it will be said locally that she has gone away."

I didn't like the sound of it, the implications, but Storvac must know what he was doing. "Where to?" I asked.

50

"To stay with an aunt in Moscow. Comrade Yasnov's sister, who exists and will co-operate."

I shook my head. "Is that going to be believed? After what we assume was the noise that must have been heard . . . and suppose you're seen, taking the body out?"

"We shall not be," Storvac said. He sounded confident. He looked at his wrist-watch: the time was getting on and outside it was as wintry as ever, more so in fact, and the darkness was intense. Once the body was on the ground floor and out to whatever conveyance Storvac planned to use, the Volvo no doubt, it would of course be easy. The danger and the difficulty lay between this flat and the entrance lobby. Storvac turned to Yasnov. "There is food, Igor?"

"Yes . . ."

"We should eat. We must keep up our strength, Igor, you and us."

Yasnov broke down then. He said in a shaking voice, "Irina cooked for me. I am useless without her." He slumped onto the hard chair in the kitchen and put his head in his hands and sobbed. It was a distressing scene; Storvac patted his friend on the shoulder and said he would cook. There was no reaction from Yasnov. Storvac rootled about and found a loaf of black bread, a tin of beans and some eggs. There was an electric stove, old and lethal-looking. Storvac found a pan in a cupboard beneath the sink, filled it with water from the tap, and put it on one of the hotplates. On another he placed a saucepan with the beans from the tin. He used the grill to toast four slices of the black bread. The hotplates took ages to gather any heat at all but after a long wait the meal was ready. During its preparation and the subsequent eating scarcely anyone spoke, each busy with his own thoughts and the pervading presence in the bedroom of that tortured, broken body. We sat around the table glumly, only the two strong-arm boys seeming to have much appetite. But Storvac made Igor Yasnov eat, insisting again that he must keep up his

51

strength. Yasnov gagged, but ate. When the meal was finished and cleared away, Storvac gestured to his thugs to wash the dishes and pans. Then he said, "Now we wait for three more hours."

I asked, "You'll use the Volvo, Storvac?"

He nodded. "It will be brought when we are ready. Not before."

"Suppose the flats are being watched?"

"By the KGB? I think not – "

"Not the KGB, Storvac. Greenfly."

"Yes, I have thought of that. So be it. There are two things we can do: shake them off when they follow, or allow them to follow and then deal with them." Once again he seemed wholly confident. I glanced across at the thugs. There was a smile on each face, a look of anticipation. They looked as though they loved shooting and were about to come alive.

I told Storvac I'd like to accompany the cortège. He seemed to understand that I would want to be around if and when Greenfly showed, and he raised no objection and neither did Yasnov, who was still sunk in his misery.

After that we sat on in silence, waiting. Every now and again Storvac looked at his watch.

Both the thugs went down to fetch the Volvo from the warehouse. One of them said they would need to fit chains over the tyres: the snow, though by this time it had stopped falling, was thick. Down they went, clumping on the stairs. Storvac, watching from the door of the flat, said the stairs were deserted so far as he could see. Coming back in, he put the finishing touches to the body, which had now been wrapped heavily in sheets and blankets and had been curled round into something like a ball, securely tied into a large square of tarred canvas that Yasnov had produced from his broom cupboard – it had been supplied by the janitor to cover a broken window and had not been returned when the window had been re-glazed some eight

52

months later. More rope was bound around the canvas. Irina had been a girl of small stature but nevertheless would be a considerable weight to carry in a nonchalant manner so that the burden would give the appearance of being no more than, say, a bundle of old clothing or such.

It would be cruel to ask Yasnov to carry it, Storvac said to me in a whisper, and he himself was not a strong man. He would stagger.

I took the hint. "Very well," I said.

"There is the cross." There was indeed. It was a modern cross, not made of wood but of some sort of alloy with screw holes, quite light in fact, and bendable. It had already been bent but I said I couldn't carry both – not the weight but the awkwardness was the trouble. Storvac said he would carry it but seemed worried. I said it no longer looked anything like a cross and shouldn't arouse any particular suspicion if seen on the way out. With the body tied up, all that remained to do was to clear up the last traces of blood, and Storvac got on with this, going around on hands and knees with a wet cloth from the sink. Then, as soon as the Volvo was heard below, crunching slowly through the snow, we left the flat and Yasnov pulled the door to behind him.

He led the way to the stairs, tears pouring down his cheeks. I prayed that no-one would be about to see. I went next, carrying my burden, with Storvac and the bent-up cross in rear. It was bitterly cold on those unheated concrete stairs, colder still in the entrance lobby with its door to the open air, the freezing air. There was light in the lobby and I could see the Volvo with its chained tyres, drawn up close to the doorway. Unobserved I carried the bundled body through and laid it thankfully in the boot, already opened by one of Storvac's men. Yasnov got into the back of the car and Storvac followed him with the cross. I got in on the other side at Storvac's request and sat there with the sharp ends of the cross biting into me: some of the bends had ended as fractures. The boot lid was shut down and locked and both the tough chaps got in the front and with no time lost we drove off. Both Storvac and I were keeping a sharp lookout for anything like a Greenfly but there was no-one at all around so far as we could see, which was a piece of luck though it would have taken a lot to get any ordinary member of the public to venture out in that freezing air. Thereafter and for a long way I kept a watch for a tail but again there was nothing. A sense of anticlimax set in. Maybe Greenfly wasn't involved after all; but if they weren't, who was? You don't get crucified by accident or suicidal intent . . . and lovers' tiffs, for instance, don't normally lead to crucifixion. I reckoned it had to be Greenfly. They just weren't on the ball, that was all. I found that strange in itself. Outfits like Greenfly, living their lives on the brink of death, are normally ultra efficient because they have to be.

As it turned out, Greenfly had been on the ball all the way through.

5

The marshlands were not so far off: about fifty miles, Storvac had said, to Mar'ina Gorka, south-east of Minsk, and then a little way beyond until we were well out in the lonely places. Not far, but the weather was against us and the thug who was driving – his name was Badyul – was taking it carefully even with chains. None of us wanted an accident, a skid off the road, with our burden in the boot. So it took time and it was after two a.m. when we passed through Mar'ina Gorka, not much of a place, lying under a blanket of snow. It wasn't the best of times to dump a body in a marsh, as Storvac realised well enough, but we would have to do the best we could, break the ice and so on and make sure that the canvas bundle vanished sufficiently not to be discovered before more clement weather allowed it to sink or be sucked down finally.

Some ten miles south-east of Mar'ina Gorka Storvac leaned forward and said, "Here we shall stop." The car came to a halt on the lonely road. I had been looking out ahead and to right and left. I couldn't see much, only where the headlights showed, and what I saw was dreary country with the shapes of scrubby bushes and stunted trees, flat and unwholesome-looking even though the snow covered all.

I said, "I suppose you know where we are, Storvac."

"Yes. Well enough."

"I assume there's marsh both sides. Do you know the safe tracks through?"

"We must take a risk," Storvac said, and got out.

55

Yasnov and I got out with him, and stood shivering in a
bitter wind from the north-east, from the Siberian wastes I
supposed. It certainly felt like it, seeming to carry the
sting of death. It was pitch dark, not a star in the sky. The
risk was frightening; one false step and whoever made it
could be in the marsh, though the big freeze might protect
him from immediate immersion in the sucking mud.

Stoutly Storvac said, "I shall lead." He was a brave
man. "Badyul, you and Belov will stay with the car. I shall
go to the left of the road. Swing the car so that the
headlights show that way."

We stood and watched as Badyul shifted the car, laying
it slap across the road. What would happen if anyone came
along I just didn't know, but supposed, or anyway hoped,
any traffic would be unlikely. I mentioned it but all Storvac
said was that the job shouldn't take long. He had the cross
with him. He unlocked the boot, gestured at the bundle,
and caught my eye.

"All right," I said. I bent and heaved the body out.
Storvac took it and hefted it onto my back. Before he shut
the boot he brought out the heavy jack. Then, with the
bereaved father, we moved off the road to the left in the
long beam of the Volvo's headlights. We moved very, very
slowly behind Storvac, who took it cautiously, a step at a
time, gradually easing his weight onto each outthrust foot
in turn. The wind whistled eerily and the cold bit hard,
right through to the bone. There was the weird hoot of
some night bird from across the marsh and the first time I
heard it I almost dropped the bundle. Behind me Igor
Yasnov gave an occasional dry sob but came on stoically.
We had gone perhaps fifty yards when there was an
exclamation from Storvac and I heard a cracking, crunching
sound. Storvac lurched and fell, cursed briefly, then picked
himself up, looking muddy and smelling terrible.

"We have arrived," he said. "This will be the place."

"Not too iced up?"

Storvac said, "Oh no. Not as thick as I feared, Commander Shaw. Some work with the jack. You may put down the – the canvas."

"Right," I said, and did so. Gingerly Storvac reached forward with the car's jack and bashed at the marsh. There was more crunching and some muddy ooze spattered horribly and there was more stench. Storvac worked away for some time until he had made a considerable hole in the thin ice cover, then he ceased operations and stood for a moment breathing heavily from his exertions.

"Now," he said. "Lift. I will help."

He did so; we lifted the bundle together and began to swing it to Storvac's orders. When we had a good swing on, he gave the word to let go. The pathetic bundle went ahead perhaps four feet and dropped into the broken-up marsh. There was a plop and a shower of filth. Yasnov stood on the firm ground, eyes shut, saying something in a keening voice, a prayer perhaps. I didn't know if he believed in any God; being part of WUSWIPP I doubted it. Perhaps he was just taking precautions against the chances of the Party dictum about 'no God' being wrong. Lenin, Stalin and the rest – they didn't have to be right all the time. The bundle was already starting to disappear, the sucking action of the marsh having its effect.

Storvac laid a hand on Yasnov's shoulder. "I am so sorry, Igor. Now we go. It is done."

"Yes, it is done, Comrade."

Yasnov turned away, his face haunted in the headlights' beam. We all turned away. A moment later I heard a scuffle of feet behind me, followed, as I turned quickly and saw the leaping figure, by another plop and a shower from the marsh. In the Volvo's lights I saw Yasnov's torso some distance from the firm ground, saw his arms reach for the vanishing bundle, saw him begin to sink.

Storvac's face was as haunted as Yasnov's had been. He said, "There is nothing we can do. It is perhaps for the best."

"Perhaps," I said. I didn't know quite which way Storvac had meant it. The best for a despairing father, or the best for us, those involved, if the KGB should ask questions about a disappearance – there would now be one man the less to perhaps break under torture.

When we turned away towards the Volvo we saw the distant lights of a vehicle coming dangerously fast along the road from Mar'ina Gorka.

Badyul had acted commendably fast. We saw the swing of the headlights away from us as he straightened the car. Now we were in total darkness. Safe from one angle, in much danger from another – the surrounding marsh. "Who d'you think it is?" I asked.

"Who can say? Perhaps Greenfly, perhaps not. You have your revolver?"

"Yes," I said, reaching for the shoulder holster.

"I too. Now we wait to see if it stops. We shall move closer meanwhile."

Slowly, very slowly, we moved. I prayed hard that we didn't literally put a foot wrong. The approaching car now had the Volvo in its own headlights. A few moments later it started to slow, then it stopped immediately behind the Volvo. I saw that it didn't carry any police insignia but that didn't have to mean much: the KGB don't advertise. Neither, it was to be presumed, did Greenfly. I wondered why Badyul and his mate hadn't scarpered, left the vicinity like bats out of hell. They were either brave and loyal, or bloody stupid. Or perhaps they knew that WUSWIPP's revenge would be as bad as anyone else's. Anyway, they stayed put, not getting out of the car as four men in dark clothing, carrying sub-machine guns, Kalashnikovs I believed, bundled out from the other car and ran for the Volvo.

They had their backs to us now, which gave us a chance if we wanted to open fire. I wasn't at all keen to open fire on the KGB and said so as I saw Storvac lift his revolver.

58

"It is not the KGB," he said softly. We were closer now. "One of them I recognise. Stefan Grulke."

"And he is?"

"A seceder to Greenfly," Storvac answered. He pointed him out, lifted his revolver again. I knew from the old days that he was a first-class shot, one of the best I'd come across. I wasn't bad myself. When Storvac opened fire and one of the men dropped and lay twitching in the snow, I knew I had to back him. I took aim and fired, and another went down. But the other two had had time to take cover on the other side of the car, and as Badyul and Belov inside reacted a stream of rapid fire came out over the marsh and we ducked. The firing was kept up for a while and when it stopped I heard a loud scream from inside the Volvo and a fraction of a second later I saw a lick of flame curl up from around the bonnet and then almost before I had time to take a breath the Volvo was a seething mass of fire, just as though a petrol bomb had gone off inside. Flames shot skywards, smoke poured, and the gunfire was resumed, sweeping out across the marsh. By now Storvac and I were both lying flat on the firm ground. No doubt making the assumption that that would be precisely what we would be doing, the gunmen kept their fire low. I heard the whine and buzz of sustained fire, saw the men outlined in the blaze from the Volvo, firing from the hip. Bullets thudded into the ground all around us. Storvac was a little ahead of me and in the lurid orange light I saw him get hit. He gave a short scream and half lifted his body, twisting in agony, and took more bullets, this time in the head, which seemed to split in half and that was that. I knew I couldn't do much good now but I lifted my revolver and fired back at the men, and missed. I missed because in the precise second that I squeezed the trigger a bullet took the revolver and tore it from my hand, and sent it spinning away. The men probably saw that; there was no more gunfire and I saw them moving cautiously out from the road towards me.

With his Kalashnikov pointed down at me, the leading man said in English, "Commander Shaw, I think?"

The car that had brought the gunmen had backed away fast from the blazing Volvo, which was now no more than a glowing skeleton with twisted frames and the remains of Badyul and Belov still sitting there with smoke drifting up from their corpses. I reckoned they'd been killed by the guns before the fire had started. It was a gruesome sight. I was marched past all that was left and put into the other car, a Lada. No-one spoke until the Lada had been turned and was heading back towards Mar'ina Gorka. Then the man whom Storvac had identified as Stefan Grulke, the one who had addressed me by name in English and who was sitting alongside me in the back, prodded me with a revolver and said, "You will have disposed of the girl, of course."

"I don't know what you're talking about," I said. "I'd be obliged if you'd tell me who you are."

There was a laugh. "Did Comrade Storvac not recognise me?"

"All right," I said. "Yes, he did – Comrade Grulke."

"So the introductions have been made. And you have disposed of the body, Commander Shaw."

"You seem to think you know it all. Why should I argue the toss?"

"There would be no point. You are not so clever as you think, Commander." Again Grulke laughed, an unpleasant sound and a threatening one. "You failed to check the Volvo. A device held underneath by suction. Most effective!"

I took a deep breath. So that was it; they'd just followed a bleep at a discreet distance, no need even to hurry. It could have been fixed easily enough after the strong-arm men had left the car. I said, "I suppose you killed Irina Yasnova?"

"Not me personally."

60

"Why was she killed?"

"A score to settle with her father – it is not important."
Grulke's voice was totally impersonal, he might have been
discussing the casual squashing of a woodlouse. "Storvac,
no doubt, told you that I am a member of Greenfly. I shall
tell you something else." Grulke seemed addicted to his
loathsome laugh; he gave it again. "Do you wish to hear?"

I'd already guessed what was coming. I said, keeping
my tone level, "I'm a captive audience, am I not?"

"Yes." He seemed to find that unduly funny. When he
had stopped laughing he confirmed my suspicions. "We
have your Miss Mandrake," he said.

"I see," I said, feeling suddenly cold inside now that I
knew for certain. "Where?"

"Somewhere."

"I'm being taken to her?"

"No."

"How do I know you're telling me the truth, Grulke?"

"I shall show you." With his free hand he reached inside
his heavy greatcoat, through to his jacket, and brought
something out. A photograph. This he held in front of my
eyes and spoke in Russian to the driver, who flicked on the
interior light. It wasn't a good light but I was able to
make out Felicity. She was lying on a floor and she was
spreadeagled as to her arms, and she was tied with rope to
a cross.

I was driven on for a long time, back through Mar'ina
Gorka after which we headed out along a road that Grulke
said led away from Minsk. There was, he said, nothing to
go back to Minsk for. The Minsk end was closed now; the
fact that I had gone there with Storvac was a bonus for
Greenfly – I'd not been expected but they were delighted
to have me. It appeared that Felicity hadn't told them
what they wanted to know, whatever that might be. I was
not immediately informed of Greenfly's wishes. But I was
told that already London was beginning to react to my

disappearance and Miss Mandrake's; also, of course, to the botched border crossing made by one of the Ladybirds. Greenfly had its men in London, Grulke said, men with big flapping ears. Both Whitehall and 6D2 HQ were playing it all down and there had been nothing in the press about disappearances. Not yet, I thought, but it wouldn't be long; of course, the shooting incident on the East German border had been given the press treatment – and the press was speculating after getting the official hand-outs. The East Germans had waxed synthetically indignant about the West assisting would-be escapers; much had been made of the presence of Hans Schulz, citizen of Braunlage in the Harz. As for Whitehall, they had categori-cally denied any involvement on their part, which was strictly true since it had been handled by 6D2. We're all of us two-faced these days, from sheer necessity. Government and the maintaining of peace has become dirty business. According to Grulke, the diplomatic furore had a long way to go yet: it had only just begun and would escalate.

"And the times are dangerous," he said. "For the West."

"Meaning?"

That damned laugh. "You will see, Commander Shaw. There is a little time yet."

I asked casually as though I'd never heard of them before, "What are these Ladybirds you spoke of, Grulke?" Arthur Webb had been so certain, back in Focal House, that the Ladybirds were on to something big, something brewing behind the Curtain, something that had made a woman risk, and lose, her life. But I didn't get any information about the Ladybirds from Grulke. He laughed yet again and made some remark in Russian to the driver, who also laughed, making a spiteful sound of it. Conver-sation died after that and I was left to think about Felicity and what she was undergoing. That cross on the floor; Grulke hadn't elaborated after he'd put the photograph back in his jacket and of course there had been no need to. In my mind's eye I could see the cross being screwed into its upright position, and the nails being driven into the flesh and gristle, and the weight coming on, and the constricting diaphragm . . . Everything was lined up ready and I wondered in an agony of my own what the time-schedule might be. Then Grulke started up again and, right out of the blue as it were, said something intriguing.

He said, "Since Comrade Gorbachev came to the supreme power in the Kremlin, the supreme *effective* power, there has been a growing movement towards a peaceful life with the West."

"Towards détente?"

"Yes. Away from confrontation."

"Why do you make that point, Comrade Grulke?"

I was reaching screaming point at his laugh. That was his only reaction to my question and he returned to silence. According to dead Storvac, it was WUSWIPP that wanted less confrontation, seeing what it was leading to and having suffered a metamorphosis of their own. Not so Greenfly. And as if in confirmation I had detected a criticism of Gorbachev in Grulke's tone.

We drove through the night; the Lada carried petrol cans in its boot and en route the car was stopped so that the driver could top up the tank. As the dawn came up, iron hard, bitterly cold with more snow in the sky, I saw that we were heading east into the rising sun. Shortly after that I was told to get down on the floor: I wasn't to see where we were going, and that must mean journey's end was not far off. I crouched on the floor, very uncomfortably under Comrade Grulke's feet and gun, the latter making sure I didn't try to lift my head for a look. When I eased my neck after a while, I got a hard tap on the head from the barrel, just as a warning. When we slowed I guessed we were coming into some sort of built-up area; and, though it was early, there were traffic and pedestrian sounds, the workers on their way to complete some quota or other to the greater glory of the Soviet Union. After a while the

Lada slowed still more, took a sharp turn, and seemed to be going down a slope. The daylight went and I became aware of the backglow from artificial lighting and of a smell of stale air mixed with petrol fumes. An underground parking lot was my guess, but it turned out to be more than that. When I was allowed off the floor, and pushed from the car in front of Grulke's gun, I got the impression, which turned out to be correct, that we were in a private car park belonging to some kind of organization, or maybe just a group of offices split up among a number of interests.

There were several cars parked, around twenty, but no persons beyond ourselves. The driver remained in the car while Comrade Grulke propelled me across towards a door, a heavy fire-proof door with a notice on it in red, a warning that the door was to remain closed at all times. Inside, there was a long corridor, concrete all around and under-foot, with light bulbs in recesses in the ceiling. The air was cold and dank and our footsteps echoed. A few years earlier, I'd landed up inside the Lubyanka prison in Moscow – we wouldn't have had the time to make Moscow on this trip from Mar'ina Gorka but this place had a similar feel to the Lubyanka with its torture cells, its interrogation rooms, its overall horrible security and sense of doom. I had to fight down mounting claustrophobia: when you've once been in the Lubyanka, in the hands of the security police, you don't want to face anything like it again.

The corridor ended in a lift and I steeled myself: I recalled the lifts in the Lubyanka – split into two halves with a steel partition, you on one side, the armed guard on the other, the lifts that brought you to the lush-carpeted corridors and the terrifying silence of the rabbit warren, not unlike Broadcasting House in its complexity of passages and doors.

We entered the lift; Grulke pressed a button and we went up fast, a stomach-sinking sensation followed by an upward surge as we stopped.

The doors slid open and Comrade Grulke laughed and

said, "After you, Commander Shaw," and prodded my backbone with the snout of his gun, and I went out into a passageway. It was a more ordinary one than those of the Lubyanka. A few people passed us, girls looking like secretaries, some male executives for want of a better word, and one or two exchanged polite greetings with Grulke, whose gun was now in his pocket – I'd seen him shove it out of sight as we left the lift, and I'd wondered why. The place had the feeling that guns would be a pretty normal sight within its portals, but on the other hand there might be a façade to be kept up.

I was halted at a door eight doors right from the lift. Grulke knocked and pushed the door open, and I was herded through into a small square office with one window looking out over a sizeable town, a panoramic view of mostly bare concrete, some of it being in the form of high-rise blocks. I had no idea where it was. A man was sitting at a desk, a squat man with a totally bald head and small, hard eyes, a swarthy man who looked as if he'd need to shave three times daily, a man built like a barrel with a wide, deep chest. He remained seated as we went in, and Grulke spoke in Russian, too fast for me to understand much of it, though I heard my name mentioned.

When Grulke had finished, the man turned towards me and stared, looking me up and down as if wondering what my pain threshold might be.

He said, "Commander Shaw." He had a high, squeaky voice, the sort I would have associated with a eunuch, and it didn't fit the body.

I didn't make any response. He asked, "Why have you come to Russia, Commander Shaw?"

I said, "I'm sure Comrade Grulke has advanced a theory."

"Comrade Grulke said you have come to find Greenfly."

"Then you have your answer," I said coolly. There wasn't anything else I could say: Grulke had known it all. So far as I could see, the whole thing was blown already.

65

What the future held for Felicity and me didn't bear thinking about too much, but it all flashed through my mind like a flaming sword, since it was simple enough: a good deal of pain for the extraction of any further information, and then Siberia, or oblivion. The West wouldn't be hearing of either of us again. I believed this squat man to be of the security police, the local big noise, wherever 'local' might be, of the KGB. Which, if I was right, meant that the KGB and Greenfly were hand in glove.

And where stood WUSWIPP? Where the Ladybirds? The squat man was still staring at me in that calculating manner, a slight smile on his heavy face now. The head was like an inverted turnip, the shining bald dome coming down to a point at the chin, rather more suddenly than a turnip – a lemon was perhaps a better simile. The smile broadened and then he said something that surprised me, initially at any rate. He said, "You do not know where you are, Commander Shaw. I shall tell you. You are in the Belaruskya Sovietskaya Sotsialistychnaya Respublika – to you, the Byelorussian Soviet Socialist Republic. More precisely, you are in the regional HQ of the World Union of Socialist Scientific Workers for International Progress in Peace."

WUSWIPP. WUSWIPP itself. I looked at Comrade Grulke. I didn't get it; not at first. Then I did. I said to the squat man, "So this is WUSWIPP territory. But you're Greenfly."

"Yes," he said.

"The worm in the bud."

The small eyes glittered at me. "I do not follow."

"Never mind," I said, "it's not important. So what comes next?"

"A period of peace and quiet," he said. "A time for reflection. And then perhaps . . . metamorphosis?"

Later, I didn't know how much later, I woke up in strange surroundings. In the squat man's office I had been held in a lock like a vice by the squat man himself. Ape-like, his arms were immensely strong. Held fast, my right sleeve had been drawn back by Grulke, who had used a hypodermic. Everything had grown hazy, just for a few seconds, then I must have gone out like a light since I have no recollection of what followed. But when I woke my mind was perfectly clear as to the present. I was in a white-painted room, very clean, clinically so; a ceiling light like an arc lamp was beamed down at me in full, eye-hurting brilliance. I was lying on what I believed to be an operating table or something similar and I was tied down to it helplessly. Ropes were drawn across my body from neck to ankles and secured somewhere beneath. I could breathe but I couldn't move any part of myself except my fingers and toes. There was a bit of a headache and a slight feeling of nausea but these passed within minutes of my coming to.

I was alone; there was no sound beyond the ticking of a clock somewhere behind me where I couldn't see it. After a while an itch developed in my left calf, a tickling about which I could do nothing except go quietly mad if it went on for too long. It grew worse. I gritted my teeth and tried to think of something else but that didn't help. 'Something else', anything else, was hurtful too: Felicity, the botching of a job that 6D2 had regarded as vital, that horrible interment in the marsh, the crucifixion, Felicity again.

The itching continued and I gave a low moan.

There was a movement behind me, a footstep: I wasn't alone after all. Someone moved into view, a girl, a nurse presumably, wearing a white overall and a white mask over her face from the nose down. Even with the mask I could see she was potentially more than ordinarily pretty – I could say beautiful. Level brown eyes, a mass of dark hair with a tiny cap perched on top, good figure – nice taut breasts beneath the overall, slim waist.

I met her eyes, and she lifted her eyebrows. What, I wondered, was the Russian for an itch in the left calf? I had no idea. I tried English; the girl spoke to me in

Russian: a fat lot of good that was! However, the itch had reached its limit; it went away and I thanked God for the relief. I could see a smile in the girl's eyes as she looked down at me, and a nod as if to herself. She moved away behind me and I heard her speaking, and when she finished there was a tinkle as of a telephone. Someone, I guessed, was being told that I had come round.

6

The squat man's name was Senyavin: Grulke thus addressed him when they both came along in response to the nurse's report. There was another man with them, tall, thin and grey-faced, wearing a long white coat like a doctor, which was what he turned out to be: Dr Kholov, they called him.

For a while all three of them stared down at me. Then the doctor asked some questions in English, purely clinical questions.

"There has been headache?"

"Yes," I said.

"Nausea?"

"Yes."

"Now gone?"

"Yes."

"There has been no other pain than the headache?"

"No other pain, no – "

"And now you feel quite well, quite normal?"

"Yes," I said.

The doctor glanced at the other two and nodded in apparent self congratulation. "As I said." He spoke in Russian but I understood that far. "It follows the pattern. He will now be feeling perfectly well and will remain so, even during the next part of the course."

Grulke and Senyavin nodded. Then Senyavin asked in his squeaky voice, "You will come to the house with us?" I understood that too. The doctor answered that he would of course come; some rapid and low-voiced Russian followed. I failed to get the gist of it but heard mention of WUSWIPP and I thought I heard the doctor say something about his being able to fix things so that he wouldn't be wanted at HQ. There was a definite conspiratorial air; my mind was busy while my body was inert and it didn't, in all the circumstances, take much cerebration to tell me that these men were using WUSWIPP to their own ends, making use so far of WUSWIPP's scientific set-up, but that at any moment now I would be removed, with them, to somewhere more private. The next step came within a few moments: the young nurse appeared again, took a grip on the fleshy part of my right upper arm, dabbed at it with some gauze soaked in something cold, and then the doctor approached with a hypodermic, pushed the needle in and pressed the plunger.

This time I didn't go out cold. I just felt numb and sleepy and very, very content, a most curious and happy feeling. I felt myself being untied from the table and rolled to one side while a stretcher was slid beneath my body and I was rolled back onto it. Then I was lifted and put on a trolley and pushed on this out of the compartment, back along the concrete corridor, the nurse at my side, and out into the underground parking lot where the doors of an ambulance gaped open to receive me. Two attendants took me over and I was lifted into the vehicle and deposited on a shelf-like bed. The nurse and Grulke and Senyavin got in with me while the doctor got in the front with the driver. I knew this because before we started off a panel slid back and the grey face looked through critically, making sure I was all right. Then off we went, bumpily. The ambulance had a tired look, not unlike a World War Two British Army field ambulance, and was very uncomfortable. Comrades Grulke and Senyavin had quite a job to keep their bottoms on the shelf-bed on the other side as the vehicle lurched and swayed on its journey:

Comrade Senyavin looked after a while as though he was about to be seasick but he managed to hold onto his stomach and, more or less, his balance. It must have been a long ride for him.

As for me, I was having extraordinary mental visions: one was of Felicity. I saw her still tied to that recumbent cross though I couldn't make out the background. Others were of Hans Schulz lying dead near the East German border, and of Frau Schulz equally dead in the house in Braunlage. Others were of London.

Max, in Focal House. Max on the line to Downing Street, sounding urgent. I heard him say, "A matter of days only, Prime Minister. My advice would be . . ." I grew hazy at that point and didn't entirely hear Max's advice but I fancied there was something about readiness of missiles and the whereabouts of the Polaris submarine fleet and a reference to Faslane on the Clyde. Then I saw a meeting of the cabinet and after that I shifted to the Defence Ministry where the Chiefs of Staff were in a tizzy.

Hallucinations. Disturbing ones, of course, but somehow I didn't care. The world was a happy place where one could relax and forget. Comrade Grulke's face, leering at me from his seat, was almost benign. Comrade Senyavin looked green but also friendly. It was a very weird feeling but I saw no danger in it. Not then. In fact I didn't until very much later when I knew it was potentially lethal. Or maybe the exact opposite: just possibly benign to the point of peaceful co-existence, the ultimate concept that would stop all wars. But not so long as the know-how was confined to Russian possession only.

When the ambulance came to rest I was taken out on the stretcher. I saw, before I was taken indoors, that I was in the grounds of a large house, something like a Black Sea *dacha* for the use of the top brass of the Soviet hierarchy. It was way out in the country, no other buildings to be seen, just snow-covered blankness and very flat, like the marshes. A dull, leaden sky, no sight of any sun, but it was still daylight, so back in the WUSWIPP HQ I had probably not been out all that long. Parked in the grounds was the Lada, with Grulke's driver just getting out of it. Probably it had followed us from the underground car park.

Once inside the house I was taken down some stone steps to a cellar, with another operating table or similar on which the stretcher was placed. This time I wasn't roped down and I had no urge to escape: my will seemed to have gone. The cellar was well lit and as clinically clean as the compartment in the WUSWIPP set-up but there was a nasty smell of what I believe was formaldehyde and this, with its connotation of corpses, I did not like but was not unduly worried. The happy feeling was still with me. In a curious way it was almost as though I was hovering between this world and the next with plenty of promise of goodies to come. The formaldehyde was there simply as an agent to waft me across the great divide, Rubicon or whatever. Or perhaps it was the Styx. But the comrades presently looking down at me had none of the terrors of Charon standing by to ferry my soul across the dark waters, though physically the bald, squat Senyavin could well have taken that dread boatman's part.

The doctor was standing at the foot of the table.

"You feel well?" he asked. "Well still?"

"Yes," I said, my voice sounding, to me, very far away.

"Good. You are very happy. You will remain very happy. You will not worry about what is to be done."

"No," I said. I think I wore a silly grin as I said it.

"There is, however, something worrying you. It is Miss Mandrake."

"That's so," I said dreamily.

"You will stop the worry, Commander Shaw. Miss Mandrake is here and is very happy too."

I said, "She's tied to a cross."

Something, a gleam of some sort, came into the doctor's eyes. He asked, "This you have seen?"

72

I was about to say yes, I had, when Grulke spoke. He said, "I showed him a photograph." The doctor looked a little put out, a little disappointed and tight-lipped. He didn't say anything further, however, but moved away from the end of the table and went round behind me and I heard some mechanical sounds, a whirr of electricity and something being manhandled. A minute or so after this both the doctor and the nurse approached me and started taping things to me, electrodes, one at each side of my forehead, one behind each ear, others, after removal of some of my clothing, on my chest, wrists, stomach and inside both thighs.

"You will not worry," the doctor said again.

"No."

"You will relax."

"Yes." I was nicely relaxed already.

"You will allow your thoughts to drift."

"Yes."

"You will not think of Miss Mandrake. Accept that she is happy, relaxed like you."

"All right," I said. The image of the cross had faded for some reason or other. It was like a kind of hypnosis although I knew it wasn't that: there was no eye work on the doctor's part, no swinging of watch-chains or whatever it is they get up to. Sleepily, I said, "I'm sure she's happy and content."

"Quite so. Very happy, very content. And also quite safe. Perhaps you will see her soon." The doctor looked down at me with a kindly smile. "Let the drift begin," he said.

"The drift?"

"The easing of the mind, the letting of the mental processes take their own course. Then we shall be ready to begin." Once again the doctor moved away behind me and a couple of seconds later I felt some gentle stinging, no more than that, from the electrodes. Quite a pleasant feeling; and I grew more and more relaxed without feeling

73

exactly sleepy. Then there was further mechanical sound and a trundling of wheels and a large square of white material, framed in metal, was pushed past me and set up in front of my table where I was able to see it. A screen like home movies . . . there were shadowy figures moving across it and as these became firmer I recognized dead Hans Schulz – of whom, for no real reason, I happened to be thinking at that moment. Then I thought of Felicity and as I did so she appeared on the screen, not on the cross but sitting in an easy chair with my London flat furniture in evidence.

The doctor was growing excited: I could see it in his face. As I thought this, he appeared on the screen, a double of his current self. I was, to say the least, intrigued but only in a very relaxed way as though none of it really mattered. I heard the doctor saying something to Grulke and Senyavin, something about a full test first, to which they agreed, and then he spoke to me again.

"You have hobbies," he said. "Things you do in your spare time, yes? Perhaps chess."

"Not chess," I said, and, thinking of the game, a chess board reflected from my mind, from my thoughts, onto the screen. Then I thought of golf: I played off four, not a bad handicap at all. The Royal and Ancient's clubhouse appeared, then the little hut by the eighteenth green. The fairways whizzed past and halted by the Admiral's bunker, so called because many years ago, long before my time, a choleric admiral had been unable to get his ball away from the sand and had had a heart attack and died in the bunker. As I thought of this, a red-faced elderly man showed up on the screen – in admiral's uniform which was ridiculous, but Comrade Senyavin jumped on it, metaphorically.

"An admiral! A British admiral! Why is this?"

I explained.

"So stupid, to become so excited about a game. Unless it is chess." But he seemed satisfied that my thoughts hadn't suddenly latched onto preparations for war against the Soviet, the immediate deployment of the golfing admiral to a nuclear-powered Polaris submarine with her missiles aimed at Moscow. That moment, of course – looking back – was when I should have ticked over as to what this was all about, but I didn't. I was too relaxed, too unworried, too comfortable and happy. More golfing scenes appeared, interspersed with drinking sessions in various nineteenth holes – Muirfield, Lytham St Annes, Sunningdale and one in Spain which seemed to interest Comrade Senyavin since Spain was once again a kingdom and had been fascist. He muttered something in English about leopards and their spots. Suddenly, one of those weird shifts of the mind that come about for no reason, Felicity and I were in bed at my London flat. The doctor gave a discreet cough but Grulke and Senyavin watched as though transfixed, mouths open above sagging jaws. To their obvious disappointment, I switched off, my drugged mind roving again, and the result was a blur of several disjointed shots of Felicity and Max and the funfair at Littlehampton in Sussex where as a child I'd been taken by my parents as a last day of the summer holidays treat before going back to my boarding school. This led by natural processes to scholastic scenes and a number of canings, me being the victim.

"Ah!" Senyavin said. He had unearthed a sexual deviation. But the doctor shook his head impatiently and went into an explanation in Russian, doubtless a lesson on the peculiarities of British boarding schools. After this, the screen went blank as my electrodes were switched off and the three men went into a huddle. I couldn't hear what they said, but I caught the nurse's eye and forgot about them. That eye had a nice twinkle and somehow it made me feel better than ever, safe and in good hands and never mind the fact that the girl must obviously be in the Greenfly camp, and before that, WUSWIPP whose hands in the past, never mind their current change of heart, had been dipped in any amount of blood.

75

When the huddle broke up, I was given another injection. "A booster," the doctor said. A booster it may have been but it felt a little different: I can't explain how. I had a weird sensation throughout my body, quite pleasant really, and my mind started doing funny things, prophetic things, as though I was looking into the future.

Then I was left alone except for the nurse. She took my pulse and blood pressure about every five minutes.

"You will think," the doctor said softly, bending over me. The electrodes had been activated again and were tingling, and the screen was once more alive and kicking. Kicking – almost literally. Shafts of light sped across, then more solid things in rapid succession, giving it the appearance of jerky movement. This went on and on; the doctor grew impatient, but I couldn't help my racing thoughts. I wasn't quite co-ordinating. The doctor said, "Concentrate, please, Commander Shaw."

"I'm trying to."

"You must not try only. You must succeed. I shall direct your thoughts again." He repeated what he'd said at the start of this second session. "You will think of London. You will think of Whitehall, and of your Prime Minister, and of the Chiefs of Staff."

"I did, earlier," I said. "In the ambulance – "

"Do so again."

"All right," I said obligingly, and for a few fragmentary seconds I did. Fragmentary was the word: the Prime Minister turned jagged like a jig-saw and the pieces slotted into Francis Pym and immediately after this the *General Belgrano* sank again and the screen showed the House of Commons and a flurry of order papers coming down in a shower on Tam Dalyell.

The doctor hissed like a snake, and stamped his foot. "He is not connecting," he said, although I didn't catch this. But I did when he went on, "It is like the woman

76

Mandrake. The result will not come. It is in their personalities."

I sensed disappointment in the air; also blame. Grulke and Senyavin were looking angry and the doctor seemed to have lost his confidence. I was sorry if I'd contributed to what looked very like a cock-up: that doctor could be on draft to Siberia if he didn't succeed in what the comrades wanted. There was a lot of Russian jabber and pointed fingers and from the sound of them peremptory orders were being issued. I got the gist of some of it: the doctor was being told to explain to me, so that given my present euphoria I would co-operate.

Looking anxious, he obeyed.

He said, "You are required to move into the future. Please do so, mentally."

"You want me to prophesy something?" I asked, puzzled.

"Not to prophesy! To record and transmit."

I said, "I don't follow. I'm not," I pointed out, "a machine." I smiled placatingly.

"But that is precisely and exactly what you now are! The drug, the injection, will have done this temporarily. You are now able to mingle with the wavelength as it were . . . the thoughts and actions currently of the people of whom you think. You are in a mental and physical state where you are a vehicle for extra-sensory perception. A kind of dream, but not quite that. You do not, I say again, prophesy. You watch and listen, and then you tell."

"What I see and hear . . . it appears on the screen?"

"Yes! Via your mind, your brain. An eavesdropping of the conscious mind. The great Socrates stipulated that in dreams the soul can apprehend what it does not know. But you do not dream, you are awake. Your mind, not your soul, is now able to apprehend what normally it does not know. The element is precognosis but of the present not the future."

"Telepathy?" I asked.

"Of a kind, yes. Induced telepathic ability. Do you now understand?"

"No," I said. I found my mind split, in fact. Part was already telling me what was really obvious, that this was a Greenfly attempt to get inside the minds of the British Government, though I didn't know for what purpose; part was telling me that the attempt was doomed to failure because this doctor had got it wrong somewhere: my mind was currently too fragmented, too diversified for any useful sort of cohesive thought-transference if that was what this was all about. The doctor had been a shade too clever for his own good and had sold his crackpot ideas to Grulke and Senyavin before they were ready, at any rate in my case and, I remembered from what had been said earlier, Felicity's as well. That was what I thought. However, the doctor was the persevering sort.

I was given another injection.

I was again allowed an electrode-free period for it to take effect, to seep through my mental system, while the nurse continued the pulse and blood pressure checks at short intervals. The feeling was a curious one, as though my mind had become detached and was being thrown about as if in a rough sea, darting here and there. But a little later when the electrodes were once again activated my mental processes steadied, just briefly: Max appeared on the screen in the well remembered background of the penthouse suite in Focal House. He was using the telephone and his face had a worried look, but that was about all. No words came through from my mind and in any case he was visible for only so long as it took him to put the phone down with a bang and then he seemed to dissolve in a curious red mist and after that there was nothing more that was any use to the doctor or the two comrades.

There was some angry discussion: I think the doctor was trying to say he'd at last got a contact, which was something; but Senyavin and Grulke both thought I had just been doing some past thinking and was not projecting

78

along the required lines. Then the three injections, perhaps, caught up with me and I drifted off into sleep. How long for I didn't then know; but when I woke I was no longer on the table but in bed in a different room and I had a throbbing headache and a violent feeling of nausea and I was retching horribly without actually being sick. But my mind was crystal clear and all the earlier events came back to me, including the knowledge that the doctor's scheme had failed and I had given nothing away via my mind, or by speech either of course since I hadn't the faintest idea of what was going on in London even if I could make a reasonable guess at a certain high degree of anxiety and uncertainty.

The nurse was there. She was no longer wearing the mask and I could see her features. These were a disappointment: she had a badly repaired hare lip. This gave her a more sinister appearance, taking into account the circumstances. Once again she took my pulse and blood pressure, made some notes on a chart, and then spoke to me, in English.

She said, "It is good. The doctor is pleased. You are a much valuable person now."

I stared back at the hare lip, feeling creeping horror. Pleased, was he? Why? There was just the one answer: what he'd failed to extract while I was awake had come through, no doubt unexpectedly, while I was asleep.

7

I had been told to get dressed: my clothes were draped over the back of a chair. The sickness was leaving me but the headache was still there. When I was dressed the nurse pressed a bell and from somewhere a disembodied voice came through and there was a short conversation. Ten minutes later I heard an electric whirr and the door of the room, a steel door, slid back to admit a man carrying a tray.

Breakfast.

"You will eat," the nurse said.

"I'm not hungry."

"You will eat. It is an order." The hare lip gave the girl a kind of hideous authority; I still wasn't quite myself and in any case it's a good principle to keep your strength up for the future even if the food makes you gag, which at first this did. There were Kellogg's corn flakes, that ubiquitous cereal, fried bacon and eggs, toast, marmalade and steaming hot coffee. Very English and very nicely cooked; I ate and felt the benefit. On the tray was a packet of cigarettes, also English: Benson and Hedges. I was immensely grateful but there were no matches and when I searched the pockets of my jacket my lighter had gone. I was pointing this out to the nurse and asking her to get on the blower again when the steel door slid aside once more and a man entered, with gun aimed.

"Come," he said.

I shrugged; there would be no point in argument, so I picked up the packet of cigarettes and went to the door ahead of the revolver, which was thrust against my backbone. We went into a passageway and up a flight of stairs. There was a big window on a half landing and I looked out into daylight and bleak desolation and snow lying thickly everywhere, with just a hint of a sun shining redly behind the overcast, doing its best to come through.

I was taken into a room on the next floor. Comrade Senyavin was there alone, no Grulke present, and no doctor. I was told to sit; Senyavin indicated an easy chair. The armed guard took up his position on a hard upright chair by the door. I took out the packet of cigarettes and asked for a light.

"Certainly," Senyavin said at once. He got up from behind a desk and walked across with matches, one of which he struck and held to my cigarette. It was heaven: I inhaled deeply and wondered how the troops would get through the next war if the do-gooders ever had their way. I felt more at ease immediately, more ready to cope with an unknown, but guessed at, situation.

Senyavin didn't waste time. He went back to the desk and sat in a swivel chair and said, "You have been helpful even though the help is negative, Commander Shaw."

"Thoughts from sleep?"

"Exactly, yes."

"Not quite what the doctor ordered." This seemed lost on Senyavin, who merely nodded abstractedly. I asked, "And the negative angle?"

"Negative in a happy sense. For us. The British are not reacting. The British do not know – what they wished to know when you were sent to the East-West border at Braunlage."

"Not even worried?" I asked, trying to probe out just what I'd been responsible for.

"Worried, yes. There is concern over you and Miss Mandrake as is natural. The body of Frau Schulz has been found, and that of her husband and the Russian woman, the defector of Ladybird. You eavesdropped on a meeting

81

of the cabinet. Your Prime Minister is worried and has sought audience of your Queen in Buckingham Palace."

"The press?"

Senyavin shrugged. A little sun struggled through and lit upon Senyavin's bald head, making it shine and reflect. "The press has been told nothing beyond the fact of a border incident – this we of course knew already."

I wondered just how much of this was the sheerest bull, mere propaganda – there was no hard information and any fool could have come up with something similar. Perhaps they just didn't want me to know the doctor's brilliant chemistry had failed, though I didn't see why they should bother. But I did sense something phoney about it. Anyway, the ball was in my court as it were: I still had everything to find out, and when I'd done so I had somehow to contrive to pass it through even if I never got out of Russia alive myself. And of course there was Felicity. I asked about her and waited with a thumping heart for Senyavin's answer.

"She is well."

"But no use drug-and-screenwise?"

"No use."

"So what are you going to do about her, Comrade Senyavin?"

The Russian smiled. The sun vanished again and his head no longer reflected. He said, "She will remain well. You may ask why. I answer that you love her."

Still the hostage angle, someone to hold over me. I didn't see the point: if Senyavin and his friends thought they could get at my sleeping drug-induced extra-sensory perceptions that was surely all that was needed? Threats or the absence of them would make no difference to what my mind latched onto – or didn't latch onto – when asleep. But you never can tell with the Russians and I put on an air of indifference. "Love's a big word," I said. "We're good friends. Both in the same line of duty – you know?"

"But there is a relationship."

82

I remembered the bedroom scene, so much appreciated by Grulke and Senyavin. That couldn't be denied, and I merely shrugged it off as if it were just one of those things that happen when a man and an attractive woman are juxtaposed. Then to my surprise Senyavin said, "Soon you will see her, Commander Shaw."

Still being non-committal I said, "Good-oh." I was the more surprised because earlier, whilst we'd been en route from the Mar'ina Gorka area, Grulke had said in answer to my enquiry that I was not being taken to Felicity. Maybe there had been a shift of plan, and somehow I didn't like the implications if that was the case. I could possibly have said more, or brought through more on the ether or whatever, during my sleep session than Senyavin had come out with. But again, why should he bother? He had me and he had Felicity and he certainly seemed to believe he had the availability of my curious link with high counsels in Britain. And, assuming the whole thing really was working, it would perhaps not be outside the bounds of possibility for my mind to be projected into the White House and the Pentagon . . . in which case I could certainly be valuable, as the nurse had said. A jewel without price, in fact. And, again assuming the viability of the doctor's drugs and what-have-you, this could be what the Ladybirds had been so keen to warn the West about. But somehow I didn't think so. I believed there was something firmer than this, something more precise, more concrete as a threat. There had been so much immediacy . . .

Senyavin meanwhile had got to his feet and was standing with his back to me, looking out of the window at the snow-covered landscape. I fancied there was more snow in the sky, getting ready to fall. And I looked at Senyavin's back, a great square of muscle buried in too much fat, and almost as a reflex action I gauged the distance for a sudden spring and a throttling grip around the short, thick neck. It wasn't on, of course; I'd be dropped by the gunman behind me before I was right out of my chair. But it was something to anticipate. As for Senyavin, he was totally unconcerned, having faith in his gunman; and after a few more moments he turned and smiled across the room at me.

"You are thinking how nice it would be to kill me."

"More thought transference?"

"No. Just a simple deduction, easily made."

"Brilliant," I said.

He was still smiling. "In the Soviet Union, we do our best, Commander Shaw. As soon you will see for yourself. A car is approaching. In it will be found Miss Mandrake."

"She's being brought here, d'you mean?"

"No," Senyavin said. "She has been here for some time. It is just that when the car stops she will be taken to it, and we shall join her. Then we go to Moscow."

It was a big black car, a limousine, chauffeur driven. The chauffeur looked like long dead Stalin: the build, the brows, the peaked cap, the moustache. Alongside him sat a watchful man, thin and perky as a bird but with dangerous eyes, a man whom I knew would be armed to the teeth and fast with a gun. There was seating for six people in the back, four on the cushioned rear seat and two on let-down jobs behind the glass of the partition. As promised, Felicity was sitting there. We exchanged looks and that was all, but she seemed unharmed, anyway at first glance. I saw the sparkle of tears in her eyes and then she looked away from me, out at the lying snow. She was sitting between Grulke and another man, an obvious strong-arm man. On Grulke's other side was another man I'd not seen before. The doctor was not with us. I was told to take the off-side let-down seat and behind me Senyavin got in and took the other one. When we were all settled, Senyavin tapped on the glass and the Stalin-like driver moved off, crunching through the snow on the tyre chains that I had seen were fitted. Since I didn't know our current whereabouts I

84

couldn't assess how long it might take to reach Moscow, but with chains fitted it wasn't going to be a fast journey.

We drove through the whiteness, mostly flat country with a few trees here and there, winter dead and looking like the whitened bones of skeletons. The windows of the car misted over and I wiped mine clear with my sleeve. For some time no-one spoke; it was like a funeral procession and I began to feel like the one in the coffin. I wondered what lay ahead in Moscow: were we to be taken, Felicity and I, to the Kremlin so that the Soviet leadership, the Presidium of the Supreme Soviet in full session, could see for themselves the wondrous invention of the Comrade Doctor? Put me to sleep and let my mind go into its extra-sensory perception routine? If I were to project faithfully, it wouldn't, presumably, be selective. The assembled comrades would see the mundane things, the daily round, me cleaning my teeth, the Prime Minister visiting a crèche, the Foreign Secretary taking his dog for a walk, along with the more gripping affairs of government.

Senyavin soon began to show signs of impatience, and tapped again on the glass, making shoo-ing motions with his hand, urging more speed. The intercom came on, the comrade chauffeur in his turn urging caution. Senyavin said something under his breath and looked savage. He turned and spoke to Grulke and I was able to follow the conversation more or less. Senyavin was saying something about the Minister of Defence, Marshal Polyansky.

Grulke said, "We have time yet."

Senyavin didn't answer, just glowered. It was getting dark already: we weren't making much progress, certainly. Just trundling along over the snow. Russia, I thought, could do with some snow ploughs but of course the land was vast and the presence of snow seemed continuous. It would take a million snow ploughs . . .

As if sensing my thoughts Grulke gave a short laugh and said, "General February, Comrade! He beat Napoleon, and he beat Hitler. But we shall get there if we use caution."

"We must go faster!" Senyavin again.

He was in quite a state. He spoke on the intercom, authoritatively, issuing orders. The Stalin character gave a massive shrug as if to say it was on Comrade Senyavin's head, and obeyed orders. We went ahead at about fifty by guesswork. The chains crunched and bit but now and again there was a spin and a sideways slide. Ahead of me, through the glass screen, I could see the chauffeur leaning forward over his wheel, even his back showing tension. We were now running along through trees growing thickly to either side of the road, and that treacherous surface could send him into a solid trunk and then Comrade Senyavin, having possibly to await rescue from a damaged car, would be sure to blame the driver notwithstanding his own orders. But he was a good driver and we kept to the track, give or take a slither here and there.

By some miracle operating in favour of Comrade Senyavin, the snowfall was holding off. As the last of the light went I'd seen the overcast with us still but it seemed content merely to threaten. Soon the headlights showed us coming clear of the belt of trees, out of the forest into open country again, and I caught the dark glimmer from a stretch of water – ice, alongside the road to our left, a big lake. It was quite close; the driver slowed, and to hell with Comrade Senyavin. He would have no wish to spin off onto the ice and go whizzing about in all directions, helplessly, until he hit something. As for me, I was wishing he would do just that: the resulting panic and chaos in the back of the car just might give me my opening.

But he didn't; he moved on, slow and cautious, feeling his way, while Senyavin grumbled from his seat alongside me. He was sweating; the car was warm, having a good heating system, and Senyavin had a strong smell of BO which pervaded the atmosphere. It was mainly tension, I think: his face was tight and he'd spent a good deal of his time looking at his wrist-watch.

When it happened, it came as suddenly as these things always do. In spite of the tense feeling in the car I was starting to drop off to sleep when the end of the world hit. There was an orange flash from in front, lasting perhaps a second only but enough for me to see earth, snow and debris showering upwards, and then the thunder of the explosion and the car's bonnet vanishing as if it had never existed at all. The partition glass shattered, as did all the windows even though I imagine they were probably bullet proof. Next to me Senyavin slumped, a jag of glass through his throat. I felt blood pouring down my left arm. There was a strong smell of explosive and then the car caught fire. The door on my right, and on Felicity's left, had burst open. I jumped out into the snow and dragged Felicity after me. Behind me came the gunman who had been guarding her, looked unfit to guard a mousehole; he was shaking like a leaf and pouring blood from the side of his chest. I believe Grulke and the other man in the back were dead already; they certainly were a moment later when the whole car went up in a sheet of ferocious, petrol-based flame. Felicity and I ran like the wind, the guard behind us, just the three of us left. The chauffeur and the thin, perky man would have been fragmented instantaneously.

"What was it?" Felicity asked.

"Land mine," I answered briefly. We'd been lucky to be in a car with a long bonnet. The mine was probably not an especially big one, but it had done what it had been set to do.

Who had set it, and why? I suspected the official stalwarts of WUSWIPP, ridding themselves of a Greenfly or two and never mind Felicity and me, that is assuming they'd known we were in that car. Meanwhile the heat was intense and I pulled Felicity down below the lip of the road, the bank of the frozen lake, and I did this just about

87

in time. From the other side of the road firing started, and in the light from the flames I saw our guard go down in a heap and lie still. The gunfire was kept up for a few seconds, spraying around the area. I heard the buzz of bullets overhead, heard them ping off the ice some distance behind.

It stopped, and there was a dead silence apart from the sound of burning car. That apart, the night was very still, very dark beyond the rim of the conflagration. I felt the drip of blood down my arm and hand, into the snow. Then I saw movement on that rim. An ambush, and the explosion most probably set off by remote control.

Figures came slowly, stealthily, into view. Figures that seemed to me to be out of history, out of Russia's past, although the sub-machine guns they held across their bodies were modern enough. It was their clothing: they were dressed in white, long ankle-length greatcoats with wide lapels and nipped-in waists, and they wore tall, odd-shaped headgear of astrakhan. Cossacks, out of the long ago, but without their horses. Beneath the hems of the greatcoats as they came closer I saw what looked like riding boots. And on their backs, looming above the astrakhan hats or caps, they carried skis and ski sticks. Somehow they didn't look like WUSWIPP.

"Soviet troops," I whispered to Felicity. "The sort that operate in snow conditions. But I don't get the whys and wherefores."

"So what now?"

"Masterly inactivity," I said. There would be no point in trying to run for it, that was obvious. Even to sneak away right or left below the bank wouldn't get us far by the time that lot fanned out, looking for survivors. Nor could we hope to live off that barren country if we did elude the troops. Wandering, it wouldn't be long before we froze to death: already the cold was biting right into both of us, through to the marrow. "We'll see what develops. The thing to do is not to scare them by any sudden movement, like a bull in a field. If they just happen upon us, they may not open fire straight off."

"I don't like the idea of Siberia," Felicity said. I knew what she meant: better to die now and quickly. We were not going to be exactly welcome inside the Soviet Union. I had Felicity in my arms and she was shivering as if she'd never stop. I held her closer, trying to give her as much of my body warmth as I could and give her hope at the same time. Her hair fell across my face, wet with snow that had dropped from the bank above. I peered briefly over that bank: the figures, skirting the still burning car, were approaching the ice, slow and cautious still. Not a word was said. One of them, presumably an officer or NCO, was passing orders by hand signals, waves and pointing, gloved fingers.

I scarcely breathed: they came up to the bank, forming a line. The officer produced a powerful torch; the beam searched along the nearer ice until inevitably it picked us out. An order came; it came, surprisingly, in a woman's voice. The line closed in on us and the Kalashnikov sub-machine guns pointed down, grim dark metal outlined starkly against the snow and the white greatcoats and the remains of the burning limousine.

Another order came and its meaning was obvious.

I said to Felicity, "Come up. We have to face it now. We might get away with it," I added though I didn't think this likely: we were on duty as it were for Britain but Max wouldn't help and Whitehall couldn't afford to get involved. Never before had I been so conscious of the lot of a field operator, right out on his/her own.

I got to my feet, taking it slow and lifting my arms above my head. As I came upright and got a better view I saw that all the troops were women . . . and again I wondered why Soviet troops had destroyed a vehicle carrying WUSWIPP, or anyway Greenfly, operatives. Men of science who must have a value to the Soviet leadership. Until now I'd been in a degree of shock: it's not pleasant to be blown up and survive only by the skin of one's teeth and then to have one's thoughts frozen by the Russian General February. But now I was getting there.

I said in English, "Women. Very unexpected if I may say so."

There was much surprise. "English?" the officer asked incredulously. "Who was with you in the car?" Her own English was very good indeed.

I said, "Comrade Senyavin, Comrade Grulke, plus gunmen. All Greenfly. As if you didn't know."

"You know about Greenfly?"

"Yes," I called up. The snow was starting again now, big flakes, a heavy fall drifting through the night. I decided the time had come to take a chance: not too much of a chance. I was pretty certain I'd arrived at the facts. I said, "My name is Shaw. And you . . . you're the Ladybirds."

The torch had been extinguished; the women clustered about us, asking questions. I told them the details of the aborted border crossing near Braunlage, I told them of the killings of the Schulz family and of my meeting with Storvac and my entry into Russia via Poland, of the crucifixion of Irina Yasnova in the flat in Minsk, her disposal in the marshes near Mar'ina Gorka. Some of this they knew already, some was news; but it helped to establish our bona fides. For her part, the Ladybird leader, who said her name was Olga Menshikova, showed me a small jewelled locket hanging from a gold chain about her neck, with a ladybird enamelled on its reverse, black-spotted red on peacock blue.

"You will now come with us," she said. It was an order, imperiously given, and I was glad enough to hear it and to obey. The Ladybirds unshipped their skis and put them on their boots and then formed up around us on the hard-lying snow. Olga Menshikova had asked us if we could ski: I said we could. She looked at my arm, which might present difficulties but would have to be borne. She turned

90

to one of the women and a long, thick woollen scarf was produced and wound round my arm and wrist, presumably to soak up any blood that might drip to the snow. We were given borrowed skis – two of the Ladybirds would make their way across the ice and rejoin us later. We were valuable, not to be mislaid. We would go in the same direction as the car had been taking, leaving the smouldering wreck behind us with the bodies. Olga Menshikova said it was unlikely there would be any other traffic along this road while the wintry conditions lasted, that it could be weeks before Senyavin and the others were found. I suggested there might well be a search along the whole route. Her answer was that the snow would deepen and there was nothing, or almost nothing, left of the limousine. Its burned out chassis, and the gunman's body, would make but small hummocks and would very soon be lost in the virgin flatness of the snowfall.

She would answer no more questions. "There will come the opportunity soon," she said.

"How far have we to go?"

"You will see."

So off we went. I'd thought I could ski reasonably well, but I was a novice beside the Ladybirds. There was an air of impatience as Felicity and I stumbled about. This was a different kind of ski-ing from the alpine slopes; more of a slither, an aid to walking on snow, like snow-shoes, and it was hard work, and I kept on stubbing the wretched skis against hidden obstacles. However, we did make progress; about a mile or so along the track Olga Menshikova signalled a left turn with her torch, and we all followed her leadership, the other Ladybirds taking firm charge of me and Felicity so that we didn't plunge sideways into danger. In some ways it was like the walk on the firm ground in the marsh. Apparently there was more water around, water that was now ice and covered by the snow which was coming down much more thickly than I had yet seen it. Mile after mile of just snow, no distinguishable features, a

91

real feat of navigation on Comrade Menshikova's part. As we continued along this formless track I was able to have a brief conversation with Felicity for the first time since we'd come together again. I told her about the photograph Grulke had shown me, of her tied to a cross. She'd been terrified, she said, but in the end nothing had happened in spite of the crucifixion threats. We went on for a long way until, perhaps an hour after we had left the vicinity of the blow up, a light appeared ahead, dim through the falling snow, and the Ladybird leader said, "Now there is not far."

"A house?"

"A house, yes. A safe house. You need have no worry." Her voice was light but crisp and she was very much in command, very cool. Earlier in the torchlight, I had studied her face. It was a good-looking face, high cheekbones, eyes that could smile but yet grow cold as ice, I fancied. A wide, full mouth and a determined chin. Dark hair curled below the astrakhan headgear. And she was tall, and moved with a swing of the shoulders, the greatcoat swirling from a narrow waist. Menshikov . . . I had some knowledge of Russian history: that was one of the many things we had to study as part of our 6D2 commitment. A Menshikov had been a general of Imperial Russia under Peter the Great and had become the guardian of the young Czar after Peter's death, only to be banished later to Berezov in Tobolsk, one of the most terrible and dreaded parts of Siberia. Menshikov had been an aristocrat; Olga also had the aristocratic look, and I wondered if she might be a descendant and, if she was, whether she and her Ladybirds had impossible ideas of leading another Russian revolution, this time back to the old ways. I had noted a touch of fanaticism in her eyes.

The light grew larger, stronger. Someone, I saw as we came up, was standing in a doorway, outlined by the light, which came from an oil lamp. An old man, bent and white-haired. He called a greeting to which Olga Menshikova responded. We all approached the doorway, removed our skis, and went inside to the welcome warmth of a blazing wood fire, the smell of which pervaded a long, low-ceilinged room. The place was a cottage, the old bent man a peasant. By the fire slept a large tabby cat, making no sign of being disturbed at our entry. Olga Menshikova and the old man talked together in Russian for a few moments, then the Ladybird leader turned to Felicity and me.

"Ivan Melensky will bring food soon. Now your arm must be attended to. I shall do this myself. Sit down."

I sat on a long bench that ran along one wall of the room; there was another on the other side, filled with the other Ladybirds, who had taken off their greatcoats. Olga Menshikova went through a door at the end of the room opposite the great fire and came back a couple of minutes later with bandages and dressings and a big black pot containing a little water, which she placed on the fire after poking at the wood to make a flat surface. She told me to remove my jacket. When I had done so she brought out a pair of scissors and cut away the shirt sleeve, clicking her tongue as she did so: there was plenty of congealed blood and more began to run as the sleeve came away.

"A jag of metal from the car," she said. "It hurts?"

"Only a little."

"Good. I think it is not very serious but must be kept clean." She went over to the fire: the water was already hot enough. She came back and bathed my arm with a piece of lint, then applied some ointment. "You may ask questions now," she said. "Such as I can, I will answer."

I had many questions to ask. For a start, I asked her how the Ladybirds had known the route to be taken by Senyavin's limousine, and the timing of the journey. Her answer was that the Ladybirds had their informers: they were no inconsiderable organization. I asked how they stood vis-à-vis the authorities, the Party and the State.

"We are good Party members," she said. I pressed her on that, but she was non-committal. I got the idea that the

State was better kept at arm's length and I wasn't surprised, taking into account what Arthur Webb had told me in Focal House about sabotage and ambushes and so on. But I sensed a dichotomy in her mind as between Party and State.

I said musingly, "Menshikov . . ."

She looked up from the tying of a bandage. "Yes?"

"There was a General Menshikov, an aristocrat of Czarist Russia."

"Yes."

"Is there a connection?"

"Yes. He was an ancestor."

"But you are still a good Party member."

She nodded. "Yes. Many years have passed since the time of my ancestor, Comrade Shaw."

"And inside Russia there are many factions – even today, even under the Soviet."

She gave me a sharp look. "What do you mean by that?"

I shrugged. "Just an observation." I was thinking of WUSWIPP acting for the State, of Greenfly acting against WUSWIPP, of the Ladybirds acting currently in the interest of the enemy – Great Britain. So far I could make sense of none of it and Olga Menshikova was being of little help; she didn't like giving much away in spite of having invited questions. I asked her more as we waited for the old peasant to bring food and she continued being non-committal. In the main, anyway; when I asked her what she knew of Felicity and me she answered openly that her organization had been passed information that we were to meet the woman crossing the border at Braunlage. Later word had come through of the abort and of my entry into Russia.

"But you didn't know we were in that car?"

"No."

"You would have tried to make contact with me at some stage?"

"Yes. Very much yes! You are our link, you are the one

94

who must take word through to your government in London."

"Word of what?"

She was putting away her medicaments now; and an appetising smell was already seeping through from the kitchen quarters beyond the door. She said, "It is too soon to tell you everything. You are still in danger. Until it can be arranged for you to leave Russia in safety, I cannot speak. You must accept this."

I said, "I've come a long way, so has Miss Mandrake, to learn what you have to tell. And I understand time was short."

"Yes. It is short. But for now you must accept. And you must trust."

"Very well," I said with reluctance. I had no option. "I'll both accept and trust."

"That is good." She gave me another sharp look. "You said nothing of value in the house with Senyavin and the doctor of whom you spoke?"

I said honestly, "I don't know. But I don't think so."

"You refer to the drug-induced visions, the extra-sensory perception and the screen?"

I said yes, I did. I asked what she thought about all that: was it genuine, was it actually viable? She laughed, an attractive sound. No, she didn't believe. It was, she said, the word sounding odd in her pronunciation, boloney. But there were those who did believe in it, and those believers were in the Kremlin. Men who were sympathetic to the aims of Greenfly, she added, and were infiltrating the decision-making of the leadership.

I asked her directly, "What are *your* aims, Olga Menshikova? What are the aims of the Ladybirds?"

I don't know whether she would have answered or not; but just at that moment old Ivan Melensky came into the room bearing food, simple food of thick soup and beans and black bread with jugs of some sort of wine, and Olga

Menshikova turned away from me, at any rate momentarily. She might have turned back; but before she could do so there was a heavy banging on the door that led out into the cold of the snow-filled night and then a sudden silence fell on us all. The banging hadn't sounded like the two women rejoining from across the frozen lake.

8

All the Ladybirds had taken up their Kalashnikovs. Olga Menshikova moved over to the door and stood to one side of it. The old man, Ivan Melensky, lifted the bar that he had set in place across it after we had all entered earlier.

Snow blew in on a bitter wind, a wind that had not been there during our journey from the wrecked car: blizzard conditions were coming up.

No-one entered. The silence continued, broken only when Ivan Melensky called out, "Who is there? Who knocked?"

There was no response. Then I saw the old man stiffen as he looked out into the darkness, and I heard his sudden exclamation.

"What is it?" Olga Menshikova asked. She moved closer, coming up into the doorway with her Kalashnikov aimed through. The old man muttered something that I didn't catch, then the woman went out into the snow. A moment later Ivan Melensky followed, and so did I, and found Olga Menshikova bending over a dark object that at first sight looked like a long parcel, wrapped in furs and tightly roped. It was a moment or two before I realised that it was a body, one that could be alive but most probably was not. The three of us lifted the bundle and carried it into the cottage where we laid it on the floor and I went back for the open doorway.

I said, "There were marks of snow-shoes. They can't be far away."

"Leave them," Olga Menshikova said sharply.

"If we can find them – "

"You will not. They will know how to lie low. And what would be the use? We have many enemies. To find a handful, for you to risk yourself for small reward – this would be stupid, Comrade Shaw. And I am in charge." She said again, "You will leave them."

I shrugged; she was probably right. The sticking out of heads didn't always pay and there could be some information to be obtained from the body. I came back into the warmth and Ivan Melensky replaced the bar across the door. The ropes around the body were cut away with a long knife from the kitchen and the furs removed. I had been right enough: the man was dead, opened eyes staring up in the flickering light from the oil lamp and the fire. I had a moment of total shock, and this must have shown in my face, for Olga Menshikova, looking at me, said, "You know this man?"

"I've met him," I said. I had indeed: the corpse was that of Radley-Bewick, our man in Moscow. "You, too, know him?"

"Yes. Comrade Radley-Bewick."

The name of Piers Radley-Bewick, Eton and Christ Church, Oxford, scarcely went hand-in-hand with Comrade. But the Ladybirds might know him only as what he had been supposed to be – a spy for the Soviet who'd got out of Britain one jump ahead of M15. But I wondered if Olga Menshikova in fact knew he had been a plant, set to grow in Russian soil for the benefit of 6D2 and indirectly of Whitehall.

I asked, "What do you know of Comrade Radley-Bewick?"

She was still a stone wall. "What do *you* know of him?" she returned.

I stuck to the cover story. "I know he spied for the Soviet Union."

"In Britain?"

"Yes," I said.

She nodded but made no comment. "We must examine the body," she said. I believe she had had a notion similar to mine, that in death Radley-Bewick might reveal some sort of a clue. It was a long shot, of course, because his killers wouldn't have been fools, but it was a routine to be gone through. The furs were removed and the clothing stripped away. Radley-Bewick had continued to dress like an elegant Englishman: well-cut grey pin-stripe suit, shirt from Jermyn Street, gold cufflinks, discreet socks, hand-made shoes. He hadn't been dressed for the snows and the wide-open countryside: he could have been killed in Moscow, in his flat. There was obvious significance in his having been brought here, to be dumped on the Ladybirds' doorstep. We stripped the body right down to the bare flesh and made a minute examination. Or I did, while Olga Menshikova went through the clothing with Felicity's assistance.

Cause of death? Frankly, I had no idea. There were no marks of violence, no gunshot wounds, nothing of that nature. There had been no crucifixion. I suspected some-thing like poison, but there was no agonised expression, no clenched teeth. Some sort of gas? There were plenty of ways. Greenfly would know them all. But so would WUSWIPP, and so would the KGB. Who was it that had got onto Radley-Bewick and discovered he was no comrade?

My examination was very thorough but Radley-Bewick had nothing to offer. Not on his body, and not in his clothing either. His pockets had been meticulously emp-tied. There wasn't even a handkerchief. We'd met a blank.

Felicity asked, "What do we do with him?"

"Put him out in the snow," I said. "With Comrade Menshikova's approval, of course?" I looked at the leader, and she nodded. Out there, he would keep if we wanted him again; the ground itself would be much too hard for decent burial. Inside, the warmth of the fire would get at him; I'm no doctor but I believed he'd been dead some time already, certainly more than just a day or two. Meanwhile there were other considerations and they had already occurred to Olga Menshikova as well as me.

"Now there is danger," she said. "Somebody knows of this place, of our presence."

"You have other safe houses?" I asked.

"Of course, yes. But very far off."

"The weather's pretty poor for movement – on both sides."

"The men who brought the body got here, and so can others, Comrade Shaw."

"Do you mean to move out, then, Comrade Menshikova?"

She smiled at me. "What would you do in my place?"

I said I'd move out. I also said that she'd been a shade over confident in calling the cottage a safe house in the first place. That was a little bitchy of me, really: nothing is ever a hundred per cent safe and the security tends not to last all that long. Moving on is always a good principle. But then she surprised me: she said the Ladybirds would stay put. I asked why and got another surprise: she said she was, as I knew, a Menshikov, a one-time aristocrat. The Menshikovs still retained some of the old ideas, notably that of *noblesse oblige*, a phrase I would never have expected to hear inside the Soviet Union. Old bent Ivan Melensky, a man of greater age even than I had suspected, was the son of an old retainer who had served a Menshikov in the days before the revolution. Ivan himself had been born in those days and Olga, last of the Menshikovs, regarded him as a responsibility and she would not let him down, would not leave him to the mercies of whoever might strike at the now very unsafe house.

"Take him with you," I said, but that she scorned. Ivan Melensky was too old. This was his home, which he had never left, which he had clung onto right through the collectivisation and other trials and tribulations of the peasantry under communism. Olga Menshikova and her

Ladybirds would remain to protect him and his home, even at the cost of their own lives. I said I could appreciate her feelings but she was acting like a lunatic in the circumstances. All that the Ladybirds had stood for – whatever that might be – was at stake. How could she, in effect, back out now?

She had an answer to that too. "There are other Ladybirds in Russia. And our part is very nearly played," she said. "Now it is up to you and Comrade Mandrake."

I looked at Comrade Mandrake in bewilderment. I spoke again to Olga Menshikova. "*What* is up to us?" I asked her. "You've not been very forthcoming, have you? Isn't it time you came clean – told us what's going on?"

She shook her head. The fanaticism was in her eyes again, the fanaticism that was keeping her to her family's concept of concern for old retainers, the fanaticism that had driven her to lead the ambushes and explosions in factories and so on that Arthur Webb had told me about. I lost my temper when she shook her head so adamantly and, I thought, so stupidly. I charged her with the ambushes and killings and asked her what the point of that had been, what she was hoping for, what all this business was about and where did Britain come into it – where did I come into it?

I got a partial answer only. The explosions had been confined to property managed on behalf of the Soviet Ministry of Defence; when I asked why the Ladybirds had attacked their own country's defensive potential she commented that the Soviet build-up was for offence and I couldn't disagree with so very Western a sentiment. I said, "So you're not acting for your country, Comrade Menshikova."

"I am," she answered. "Our people do not wish for war. We do not wish to see our land attacked with nuclear weapons."

"You speak of your people. What about your leadership, the men in power in the Kremlin?"

"They are of two minds, Comrade Shaw. It is Greenfly that is for war, and Greenfly has support in the Kremlin, among the wild men."

I felt maybe we were getting somewhere at last, and I pressed, but she would say no more on that point. She turned the subject onto the ambushes in which troops had been killed. "The Ladybirds did not do that, have never done so. We were tarred with someone else's brush. We are easy scapegoats." She gave a rather bitter smile. "We are women. For women, it is much the same whether you are East or West."

"Who do you suspect, then? Greenfly?"

She shrugged. "I do not know. I think not Greenfly. And it is of little consequence . . . it could be the KGB, using all means of discrediting us."

"Have they ever used more direct means, Comrade Menshikova?"

"Oh, yes. Many times. Killings, arrests with no trial, banishment to Siberia . . . we have lost so many of our number."

I carried on probing, or trying to. Olga Menshikova stood firm. All she would say was that I must leave the cottage: I was the important one. I had come into Russia. I must leave again with the information that was to be got safely into Britain. I could do no good by remaining with the Ladybirds now. I had to move on. To move was going to be dangerous, she said unnecessarily. That was why the information could not be passed to me yet. In any case there were documents that were not in her possession. I asked her where these documents were. She refused to say precisely; I was angry but I understood. That was the way things worked, in the interest of security for all. As for contacts, you knew two people only: the man – or woman – ahead of you in the hierarchy, and the one behind. The Soviet Union was no easy place in which to live, still less in which to oppose the State or a part of it.

She gave me an address in Moscow, and a password;

also a name – Katrina. It was a code name. I must make contact with Katrina, of whom she gave me a description. She'd be found at the given address. Olga Menshikova would provide us with one of her women as a guide to the main road that led to Moscow and then we would be on our own. After this we made immediate preparations for departure. While I'd been talking, the two women whose skis we had borrowed had returned from across the ice and old Ivan Melensky had served the food and primitive though it was, it was good and nourishing and it gave us as good a start off as possible. Of course, my revolver had been removed from me back at the house where the ESP sessions had taken place; Olga Menshikova offered us a couple of small, strippable sub-machine guns, machine-pistols would have been a more accurate term. They were reasonably light and concealable and I said I would take them gladly but would ditch them if they looked like compromising us and we would go unarmed thereafter. She gave us some ammo and then as we were strapping on the borrowed skis, the Ladybird leader spoke of the dead man.

"Comrade Radley-Bewick," she said. "He had, I think, come close to the facts perhaps – "

"Which was why he was killed."

"Yes."

I nodded; I'd got her point. "He'll have had friends. Do you know who they are?"

"No," she said. "Except Katrina." Again I understood. You had to be very careful about friends. But there were, nevertheless, friends and friends. Radley-Bewick would have had some, women perhaps, who were apart from his work. They could be useful to me now, but Olga Menshikova still had no more names to offer.

The journey was a daunting prospect. Moscow, I was told, was around two hundred miles to the east. But for one useful fact it would clearly have been an impossibility, for we couldn't hitch lifts even if any traffic was moving; and we couldn't walk it within the shortening time-scale. But, Olga Menshikova said, a little over a mile to the east along the main road to Moscow we would pick up the railway line that ran from Biala Podlaska in Poland, through Minsk and Smolensk and Gagarin to Moscow. There was a bridge where the line crossed the Dneiper; and because of work in progress all trains slowed to a crawl as they made their approach. Each night a goods train ran and would reach the bridge at approximately three a.m. We would have plenty of time to reach the bridge before the train. It should not be impossible for us to swing ourselves up onto one of the couplings and then find a way into a truck, some of which would be open ones with tarpaulin covers. We would have to disembark before arrival in the Moscow terminus but that also, if risky, should not be impossible. In any case, it was the only way. Before we left the cottage, Olga Menshikova provided each of us with a heavily quilted anorak, light but warm. Then she took us each by the hand and wished us luck. We were going to need both that and the anoraks. The cold was wicked as we went out into the snow, a cruel contrast to the warmth in that old-world, lamp-lit room. The snow had stopped again, but the last fall had been heavy, and Radley-Bewick was no more than a slight hump in the white. I thought of him as I had known him: I'd not seen much of him but I'd liked him well enough – a sad man, as such expatriates as he always are, with a trustful look about him, not unlike a favourite spaniel. Maybe he had been trustful once too often . . .

We slid over the snow, pushing on our skis and ski sticks, following the guide. We reached the road quite soon, and took off the skis and handed them back: we wouldn't want to be cluttered with them when we reached the railway line. The guide waved a farewell and turned away, back to the cottage. I was sorry to see her go: it was a lonely feeling, in the heart of Soviet Russia, in the snows of winter.

We crunched east along the road. Felicity was shivering; I could almost hear her teeth chatter.

"Keep moving as fast as you can," I said. I was thankful for the hot soup that was inside us but its effect wasn't going to last. The only hope was that, if we picked up that train, we would be able to get into a truck. If we had to cling to the couplings for long, we would freeze, literally. Olga Menshikova had said the train was due into Moscow at 6 a.m. We would hope to get off in the outskirts and walk into the city. Unmolested? By the time we got there we would very likely be dirty and bedraggled, but the idea, to cover my rudimentary Russian for one thing, was to pass ourselves off as English tourists. If anyone asked for identification, we would have had it.

It seemed a hell of a long way to where the road picked up the rail track, much longer than Olga Menshikova's estimate. However, we made it and found the workings, the repair job, as deserted by any living thing as we'd been told to expect. There was just a set of signals: single track bridge-crossing was in operation, and the signal for Moscow stood at clear. I looked at the luminous dial of my watch: Senyavin's men had left me with that. It was only 2·05 a.m. Almost an hour yet to go. We crept into the shelter of a workman's hut and Felicity collapsed onto dirty wooden boards. It wasn't really very much warmer than the outside air but it least it would help if the snow returned. As it happened, it didn't.

"This is bloody impossible," Felicity said with feeling. "We'll never make it."

"We'll make it all right," I said, trying to convince myself. "When we get to Moscow – " I broke off.

"When we get to Moscow – what?"

I laid a hand on her shoulder and whispered her to keep quiet. I'd heard a sound, faint, but unmistakable. Not the train's approach: someone was outside.

9

Felicity whispered, "The men who brought Radley-Bewick, do you think?"

I said, "Probably." Before leaving the cottage and the Ladybirds I'd had in mind the chance that the corpse bringers could be somewhere around still and I'd determined that if we were attacked then I would use the guns Olga Menshikova had given us and thereafter take my chance of leaving possible KGB operatives for dead inside Russia. As it had turned out, there had been no sign of anyone en route. Now it began to seem as though they'd bided their time, seeing the railway bridge as a likely enough contact point. But it didn't have to be them. All I could do was wait and see.

After that first faint sound there was silence for a while, the silence of the grave under the lying snow. I wondered, as I waited for something to happen, how the snowfall would have affected the train schedules. All the engines would be equipped with snow ploughs as a matter of routine in the Russian winter; and since the Russian winter was an annual event, each year as harsh as the next, due account would always be taken of the snow, unlike in England where everything went haywire at the first hint of freezing conditions. It would have paid better for Senyavin to have taken the train, if only he could have done so with Felicity and me as his prisoners . . .

The sounds came again: nearer this time. I slid my gun forward, covering the entry to the workmen's hut, covering the wooden door. I could not identify the sounds: obviously

106

not footfalls, which would never have been audible on the thick snow. The squeak of a boot was the best I could think up – something leather, anyway. But if whoever it was knew we were in the hut, surely he wouldn't just fling the door open so that he would be silhouetted against the snow's white, the perfect target for anyone inside? He could be relying on the element of surprise, now lost though he wouldn't know it. That, and a fast traverse of a sub-machine gun to fill the hut with a lead spray.

I looked again at my watch: 2.15 now. If the originator of the sounds just stayed outside until the Moscow-bound goods train was heard, that would be all he needed to do. No risks for himself: he would simply bring us down after we emerged, lying hidden and firing at our backs, as we made for the bridge.

I whispered these thoughts to Felicity, my lips close against her ear: her hair tickled my nose. I said, "I'm going to sneeze."

"Oh God, no!" It was a prayer.

I held onto that sneeze; the effort was superhuman. I shoved my handkerchief against shut lips and pressed with my tongue against the roof of my mouth, the latter ploy an old trick taught me by my mother when as a child I was seized with sneezing fits in church. When the sneeze subsided I whispered, "I'm going for the door, Felicity."

"Do I come too?"

"No. Stay right where you are."

"Watch it," she said. I moved away from her, very slowly, very carefully, feeling my way with one hand while I held the machine-pistol with the other, reaching out with each foot in turn so that I didn't knock over any of the clutter inside the hut. The door was shut, not locked of course, on a sort of latch, a wood batten held at one end with a screw and the tongue slotting into a recess in another piece of wood, workable from inside and out. I reached, or rather fumbled in the dark, for this batten, all set to fling the door open and use my own surprise tactic.

107

As I touched it, I felt it rise against my hand. I'd had half a hope that the intruder might turn out to be some kind of animal seeking food or shelter but now that hope was gone, and there was only one thing for it.

I stepped aside and with my free hand flung the door open then fired a burst into the night, weaving the gun from side to side. At first I saw no man but then I saw the indentation in the snow and the black thing filling it. Then I heard the chatter of an automatic weapon away to my right, and I flung myself down. I heard bullets thud into the wooden walls of the hut. I used the gun again, weaving to the right, a long burst and then another just to make sure.

I gave it a couple of minutes, during which I thought of Felicity. There was silence from the hut. Dead, or still obeying the last order?

After the two minutes I got slowly to my feet.

No firing.

I looked down at the black form in the snow. In point of fact it wasn't all black, there was a garment like a white sheet over the clothing, but against the snow's virgin whiteness it looked dark, and some of the dark was blood. I pushed at it with a foot and it sogged but made no movement. Then I went into the hut, calling softly for Felicity. "All right?" I asked with my heart in my mouth.

"All right," she said. "Just a near miss. Who was it?"

"God knows," I answered, feeling the lifting of a great weight. "I'll go and find out. Or try to."

I went outside again. The time was now 2.25 a.m. I bent down by the body, there in the darkness. I had no means of seeing – no torch; all I could do was feel. The presence of a beard proved the sex. There was a lot of bulk, a lot of fat. The clothing was not a uniform so far as I could make out, but then the KGB – say – wouldn't be likely to be wearing uniform on a mission such as this. I felt around in the pockets and found a wallet plus the usual clutter of any man's pockets. The clutter I left, the

108

wallet I took. Also a long envelope that was in the same pocket. I moved off to the right and found two more bodies, both dead. There was nothing of interest in their pockets. I went back to Felicity.

I said, "I have some bumph. When I also get light – well, then we'll see. Maybe."

"How long now before the train?"

"Half an hour," I said.

It was a long half hour, and it was in fact longer than half an hour, before we heard the distant chug and rattle and clank of the approaching engine with its trucks.

"Out," I said. "And keep in the lee of the workings so far as possible." Together we made our way to the railway line itself, heading for a spot about a hundred yards short of the bridge on the Smolensk side. Here canvas tarpaulins had been rigged close to the track, tarpaulins as stiff as iron from the bitter cold. I could only guess that their purpose was to provide some sort of shelter for the labour gangs. Now they made good shelter for us. We heard a series of bangs as the engine slowed for the bridge and each of the trucks crashed into the buffers of its next ahead, the speed coming right off so that the train, as it came up to where we waited invisibly, was almost stopped. It was a good old steam engine out of history, a train spotter's delight, a big chugging monster with a great furnace flaring into the night and two comrades on the footplate, both of them with all their attention concentrated ahead on the bridge. I could see them clearly in the light from the furnace. Slowly the engine moved past us; I allowed it and the tender to get some distance ahead before I said, "Now!"

Some open trucks were moving past us. I had no idea what their loads might be; from low down it was impossible to see anything that might be protruding above the sides. We moved along with the train, which was still going dead slow, and swung ourselves up onto one of the couplings,

and sat astride a set of buffers, uncomfortably, dangerously, legs dangling and hands grabbing for any hold that
was going. Still the train moved slowly, giving us a chance
to settle, though I wasn't going to settle for long. We had
to get into a truck, get cover over us.

"All right?" I asked.

"Just about."

"When the speed comes on, hold tight."

"What do you think?" she responded. She was doing
her best but sounded, not surprisingly, dead scared. I
didn't believe we could make it if we stayed long on the
coupling. If we hadn't had thick gloves supplied along
with the guns and anoraks by Olga Menshikova, our hands
where they gripped the metal protuberances would have
frozen and left skin behind if we'd pulled away. I thought
about the machine-pistols which we still carried. I didn't
fancy taking them right into Moscow even stripped down
but had not been prepared to leave them at the bridge with
the bodies and risk them being traced back to the Ladybirds in the little cottage. They would have to be dumped
somewhere along the route into Moscow but until that
time came they were of some comfort. Once we were across
the bridge and gathering speed I stood up on the coupling
and, holding tight against the train's swaying motion,
clambered up the front of the next truck astern to take a
look: I hadn't done this during the slowing period since
there would be a guard's van at the rear end and the guard
could well have been keeping a lookout ahead as the bridge
was negotiated. But now, I thought, that guard would be
back in the warm. The truck was covered, as I had already
seen from the securing lines – a tarpaulin, hauled taut and
thick with snow. Not so taut that I wasn't able to get some
slack on the ropes by twisting with the barrel of the
Kalashnikov; and working patiently though with numb
fingers that prolonged the job I managed to lift a corner of
the tarpaulin and then extend the lift so that there was just
about room to squeeze through and take a chance on what

110

we landed amongst, and take a chance also on whether or not there was room. I believed there was; the tarpaulin had a sag that told me the truck wasn't fully laden.

I climbed down again to the coupling and told Felicity what to do. I said, "I'll be right behind you. Just hold tight, get your bottom on the lip of the truck, then get your legs in and let yourself down. After that, crawl clear of the gap to leave room for me. All right?"

She nodded but didn't speak. I could feel her fear, the fear that she would let go and fall, and drop beneath the wheels of the train, which, though its acceleration was not all that great, had by now gathered a fair amount of speed. But I knew she had the guts to overcome her fear: a case of teeth gritting and she was good at that.

And she made it safely. I watched her sit for a moment on the edge of the truck, a shadow in the night, then she slid down inside. I lost no time in following her. There was in fact plenty of room. It wasn't what you could call warm; but it was a lot better than the swaying, grinding buffers and at least we were out of the wind made by the train's speed.

"What's the load, I wonder?" she asked.

"Boxes. Wooden boxes."

"Crates?"

"Not quite the feel," I said, after searching around.

"That's what I thought."

There was of course no light; I wanted badly to look inside that dead man's wallet and read the contents of the envelope, but I would have to wait. I did a little more feeling around the so-called boxes. Cased guns or ammunition? I didn't think so. The shape was wrong. Too long, I'd have thought, and the wood was polished. And on the tops, on the lids, my fingers found metal plates.

I said, "They're coffins."

Felicity gave a gasp. "Tenanted?" she asked. I didn't know the answer to that, and I wasn't going to pry. But it made the journey that much more gruesome.

★

According to Olga Menshikova the train was due into Moscow at 6 a.m. That must mean we would have no daylight all the way: the winter dawns in the Soviet were late. But there would be lights to show us when we were starting to approach the capital and I would have to assess the moment to leave the train. That could not be while it was travelling at any real speed. And there would be stops at Borodino and Dorokovo only. Too far off Moscow.

"How far off?" Felicity asked.

"Dorokovo's about fifty miles, give or take."

"Might be safer?"

"I don't fancy the open road." I spoke through chattering teeth: the night cold struck through the thick quilted anoraks, almost freezing thought as well as bodies, and thought of bodies directed my mind again to the coffins on which we lay. An escape route? If they were empty . . . but an escape to where? Some Soviet funeral parlour, probably. Or maybe inside the Kremlin walls themselves – the Russians had had a run of elderly leaders not so long ago and they could have decided to stockpile coffins for future use. If it was to be an ordinary funeral parlour we might have a chance, since it's always easier to break out than in, but of course it wasn't on because somewhere along the line some busybody – right word? – would be sure to note that two of the coffins were heavier than the others and no English tourist could talk himself out of that one . . .

The train ground on, rumbling, clanking through the night, occasionally emitting a steamy whistle for no apparent reason. It wasn't travelling very fast; possibly the snow was causing delay in spite of the plough ahead of the engine, throwing the stuff aside to clear the track. A heavier than usual fall, perhaps, and our arrival would be late, which could mean some unwelcome light in the sky.

As my watch moved towards 6 a.m. I kept a discreet lookout, sticking my head through the lifted corner of the tarpaulin. I reckoned we were going to be late: we seemed

112

still to be in open country, way beyond the outskirts of any city let alone the great metropolis of Moscow. I came down again to the comparative comfort of the coffins; a wind had come up, a very bitter one, and my face and head were half frozen after a few minutes. I gave it another quarter of an hour and then I looked out again, and fancied I could make out a loom of light in the distance ahead. Thereafter I remained at my post and within the next half-hour it became obvious that journey's end was not far off. I dropped down and warned Felicity.

"Any time now. As soon as we begin to slow."

It was still dark and I was thankful for it. We wouldn't have had much hope in daylight.

It was ten minutes later that the train slowed to a crawl.

I didn't jump the gun and it was fortunate that I didn't. The crawl grew slower and then the train stopped. "Now?" Felicity asked.

"Hold on," I said. I don't know why; it was something instinctive, a hunch, no real reason to delay what we had to do. Then just a few seconds later I heard voices, and footsteps coming closer to the truck, and then a lot of banging front and rear and cursing as heavy gear was manoeuvred about, and then the sound of the engine chugging away and obviously, since we didn't move, leaving us behind.

"They've uncoupled us," I whispered. We waited: it was all we could do. Soon there was more sound, that of an engine – a shunting engine, I guessed. More bangings from the front only this time as we were coupled on, and an authoritative voice, giving orders. I stiffened as I heard those orders: my Russian, and Felicity's, was equal to the occasion. I whispered, "Did you hear that?"

"Yes. Siberia."

Coffins for the prison population, those who had succumbed and over the years ahead would succumb to the harsh and terrible conditions of the Siberian plain. As if sensing my thoughts Felicity said, "Do they give them coffins? Not just mass graves?"

"I don't know," I answered. "Perhaps they like to do things properly . . ."

"What about us, for God's sake?"

A touch of hysteria? Not likely with Felicity; but she was clearly in a high state of anxiety which wasn't surprising. All I could say was, "Hold on, Felicity. We have to wait. That's all there is to it. I've a feeling they've unhitched us fore and aft – we're on our own behind the shunting engine – "

"Just a guess."

"Yes, but a good one. And I'll make another: they won't take just one truck to Siberia. We'll be coupled onto another train. That gives us a bit of leeway, right?"

"You hope," she said bitterly.

"I do indeed," I said, and heard her blow an angry breath down through her nose. As I had said, there was nothing we could do but wait and see which way things went. I believed our chance might come during the wait for the fresh train, the Siberia express or whatever – the coffin special, perhaps. We would be shunted into a siding . . . but then again we might not be. We might be coupled up at any moment and started off on the long haul to the far north-east of the Soviet Union, the parts where the wind blew always, bitterly from the frozen seas across the frozen plain, the part of Russia where English tourists certainly didn't go any more than they emerged from coffin trucks. One thing was sure: I would take any risks to get us off that train before it was too far out of Moscow. And as always the clock was in charge: I had to get us away before the day came. Currently it was just the weather, the iron hard sky and the overcast, that was stopping the sun's light from coming through.

Snow came into the truck, blown on the wind that lifted the freed corner of the tarpaulin – which, strangely perhaps, hadn't been noticed. Soon it might be; there could be further checks before the train for Siberia pulled out. Or possibly we could both have misunderstood. It was possible that the truck was after all destined for unloading here in the capital and the railwaymen were not bothering with securing lines that had come adrift. If that was so, then we could be discovered at any moment and the sooner we broke out the better.

I had to consider the crew of the shunting engine. It was good that the snow had come back, but the fall was unlikely to be enough to shield two figures emerging through the corner of the tarpaulin and making a run for it; though the sight of living things coming out from a load of coffins might put the enginemen off their stroke for long enough, it wasn't a risk I could take.

We had to go on waiting. Here in a Moscow marshalling yard or whatever, with the shunting engine right ahead of us, I couldn't risk even looking out. And we had to keep dead still in case any movement, any sound brought someone to investigate.

"Have you," Felicity whispered in my ear, "any idea where we are?"

"Probably somewhere outside Kiyevsky station."

"How far out?"

"I've no idea," I whispered snappishly. Just at that moment there was a chug from the shunting engine, a long whistle, then a heavy jolt and we were on the move again. We moved slowly, clanking over points. It was unlikely, I thought, that we would be entering the main Kiyevsky railway station; we could go to a siding for the train to Siberia to be linked up, if we had overheard correctly, or for the unloading operation if we'd been mistaken.

It was time to go, whatever the risk. I had started to say as much to Felicity and tell her I was going to take a preliminary squint out through the tarpaulin when we stopped again and I heard the sound of what I believed was a man jumping down from the engine. Footsteps approached and then I heard someone getting onto the coupling.

10

I was already in position immediately beneath the lifted corner of the tarpaulin. Now I aimed my gun towards it. It was clear enough that the man was coming to re-secure the cover; I hadn't to let that happen. From inside the truck I wouldn't be able to loosen the ropes that passed through the eyelets in the canvas and I had no knife nor anything else I could use to cut a way out. This was the time for action.

I made a small sound, a heel on the wood of the nearer coffin. I heard a sudden exclamation and the scrabblings on the coupling and buffers stopped. There was some hesitation and then I heard the thump of a body against the front of the truck and a gloved hand appeared over the lip. The man was about to look in just in case some of the cargo had shifted – that was probably all, but he got one hell of a shock when his face came over the corner and I jabbed the barrel of the machine-pistol into it.

In Russian I said, "Stay where you are, Comrade. And don't call out."

I couldn't see his face other than as a dark blob: I couldn't see the expression. It was still dark and the snow was still blowing in past the Russian's head. Suddenly that head dipped down: he was about to run for his life, but I got to him first, dropping the gun and thrusting upright fast, using the coffins as a base, and reaching down for the hair, which was long and thick. I pulled him up by the roots and there was a terrified squeak before I got my hands around his neck and tightened my grip to near

116

strangulation point. Whilst doing all this I had taken a quick look around: there was no-one else about. The shunting engine, which was a diesel job, had only this one man as crew and we were alongside a deserted, half derelict platform with a wall behind it and a roof high overhead. I had an idea that the wall was in fact the perimeter of the railway yard and on the other side I would find an ordinary street, perhaps with warehouses, perhaps with railway workers' dwellings. To find out I hoisted the man up by his neck. He was not a big man and I was able to drag him into the truck fast enough. Once in and my hands off his neck, Felicity's pistol jabbed into his back and he gave another startled bleat. It was an eerie situation; none of us could see each other and we were surrounded by coffins.

I said, using Russian again, "One sound and you're dead."

He got the gist even if I hadn't got it quite right. He spoke in a shaking voice and I couldn't understand a word so I cut him short. I said, "We want to get out of here. Out of the yard. You're going to guide us. And we don't want to meet anyone on the way. Have you got that?"

Once again he seemed to get the drift, and said so. I said, "Right. No time to waste now. I'll get out first, then you. The lady will be right behind you." It was going to be dangerous, very tricky, and it would be a matter of luck if we got clear without meeting anybody. But I knew the fear of God was sitting heavily on our captive comrade's soul and he would show us the fastest and easiest way out. Our anoraks were roomy and we would be able to keep the guns concealed beneath them. On the other hand, I didn't want to take them into Moscow, where anyone is liable to be stopped, questioned and searched at the drop of a hat and for no particular reason. It might be better to leave them in the truck, link arms with our guide and all move through the yard as old mates, something like that . . . but then I remembered the bodies back by that bridge, who would be discovered any moment now when the workers

117

turned up for duty. There would be that link with Olga Menshikova and her gallant band of Ladybirds. I had still to bear that in mind, so we left with the guns intact.

We went along the platform. Snow blew in beneath the roof: its height provided poor shelter when the wind blew as it was blowing now. Snow had drifted up by the wall, and was lying along the track as well. There was no-one about and in the event it was dead easy: at the far end of the platform a door was set into the high wall, and our guide produced a key and opened it. That was all. We walked through into a snow-whitened roadway with warehouses opposite the railyard wall, and the Russian driver lost no time in shutting and locking the door behind us.

I visualised him scarpering at speed for authority. On the other hand, he just might not – he might keep mum. He hadn't exactly acted as a hero of the Soviet Union and he could face Siberia, even one of those coffins, if ever he confessed.

It was desperately cold and now we were hungry. We walked fast to the end of the warehouses and then turned right because it was the only way to go. Soon we plunged into a maze of streets containing high rise flats, workers' flats, all concrete and no charm, flat faced, utilitarian and forbidding. There were lights in windows and we saw children and mothers in the lower storeys; the fathers were probably already at work or on their way. People passed us, heads down, hurrying through the snow, mostly taking no notice of us, though those that did looked with curiosity: despite the Russian anoraks we were plainly not an integral part of the local scene.

"We have to get out of this area," I said to Felicity, "and not just to get away from the railway yard. We're sticking out. Tourists won't be coming down this way much." I thought of the guided tours for foreigners, the earnest persons, women largely, who shepherded the curious around and moved them on before they became too interested and asked awkward questions. Where the workers lived would not be on the itineraries: Moscow had more splendid things to show – the A.S. Pushkin State Museum of Fine Arts on Volkhonka Street; the State L.N. Tolstoi Museum; the USSR State Museum of Revolution; the USSR Exhibition of Economic Achievements and a lot more besides. I recalled the Intourist blurb: Moscow had more than 150 museums, a bumper day out for bored children. Thirty theatres, plenty of cinemas, palaces of culture and concert halls. It was around those cultural parts that we had to be. There was just one snag: I was lost. I had no knowledge of this part of Moscow. And I wasn't going to ask the way. We would have to follow our noses to the centre and then find Rybinsk Street, which was where Katrina lived. I knew more or less where that was: a side street off Baumanskya Street on the north-eastern side of the city. A long trek . . . as we passed another high rise block an old crone dressed in seedy black leered from a bottom window, grinning toothlessly and chewing her lips, the grin seeming to say, sooner you than me. We walked on fast through the appalling snowfall and as we came past a railway station and I saw that it was the Kiyevski I realized that our truck had been uncoupled some way farther west, presumably back in the freight yards some distance from the main station.

We had walked for a long time, an arduous and hazardous trek. Beneath the snow was thick ice; around us the buildings carried more ice that would slip dangerously when the thaw came. We still carried the Ladybirds' guns; there had been nowhere to dump them. You couldn't go up to a rubbish bin even if we'd seen one and produce a couple of machine-pistols and casually shove them in. But by this time they were stripped down which made concealment a little easier: we had found some toilets, a ladies and a gents – few and far between in Moscow – and we'd gone into the cubicles. Everything was iced up; and the lights had been vandalised, which didn't help, and also meant that I couldn't read the letter and the contents of the wallet I'd removed back up the line. Anyway, from now on we would at least be able to sit down without a barrel appearing in the necks of our anoraks at an inconvenient moment.

Felicity said she was hungry.

"So am I," I said. Once we had come towards the centre, all that culture, we saw eating places. But I still considered the risk too great, even though English tourists could be presumed to eat. There was no point in sticking our necks out at this stage. I said mendaciously, "Not far now. We can eat when we get there."

That was when we saw the cop looming through the snow. I felt the increased thump of my heart but the cop didn't even look up as we went by. He had a fed-up, miserable aspect as he trudged along, hating his snow-filled day. I had a fellow feeling. We went on past a magnificent building the other side of the Borodinski Bridge over the Moscow River – we should have been much farther on but I'd taken a lot of detours back beyond the Kiyevski station, some by intent, some by mistake. Felicity asked, "What's that?"

"The Ministry of Foreign Trade."

"Oh."

Farther on as we came along Volkhonka Street towards Borovitskaya Square I said, "Don't look now, but there's the Kremlin. See it?"

"Yes," she said, and I sensed her shiver. The snow lay thick, the silence that it brought held sudden menace as the high, blank walls of the Kremlin rose ahead of us, the many towers standing like anti-Western sentinels to keep out the taint of capitalism. There was something awesome about the white-covered starkness: in there was world power, in there were the men who could keep the peace or break it in nuclear thunder and destruction, and the imminence of something like that struck me more forcibly than ever. WUSWIPP and Greenfly and the Russian leadership in the Kremlin . . . what was going on in those men's minds?

Perhaps, when the meeting with this Katrina took place, I would find out.

Suddenly Felicity gave a giggle and I asked her what she found funny.

"Russians," she said. "Not the ordinary Russians. The leadership. All those grim faces, all the lack of normal humanity – men like Molotov and Stalin, Bulganin, Gromyko, Andropov. You can't imagine them doing the humdrum things of life."

"Like what?"

She shrugged. "Oh, you know what I mean . . . getting tight, enjoying themselves – "

"I can. Remember Kruschev?"

"There's always the exception. I can't imagine them, well, fornicating. Going to the lavatory. Taking the kids for a walk. Having a nap after lunch. Forgetting to post a letter. I bet they spend all their time planning production norms and going round all those dreary museums. When not planning war, that is."

"They're not all bad," I said. I was thinking of Gorbachev. He seemed human; he had quite a twinkle in his eye when seen on television – not always, but sometimes. I could see him doing all the things Felicity had mentioned. In fact I rather wished I'd thought of him when I was in the hands of those ESP boyos back west of Moscow. It would have rocked them if they'd seen the Comrade Chairman stripping for action . . .

We skirted the Kremlin. The streets were busy now, at any rate with pedestrians. The traffic was thin, by London standards of rush-hour non-existent. Somehow that added to the feeling of gloom and doom. We went by way of Manejnaya Street and Red Square into 25th October Street, past the Monument to Dzerzhinsky and the Central Post Office, glad to leave the looming Kremlin behind.

121

But I had a strong feeling I hadn't seen the last of it. I turned to look back from the vicinity of another monument, this time to Griboyedov. Felicity asked, "What is it?"

I told her.

She said, "I feel the same. Are we going to come out of this?"

I just shrugged: if I said yes she would know I was only pushing out the encouragement. We turned again, and walked on.

Rybinsk Street was, like back by the freight yard, largely high rise flats but of slightly better quality – not a lot but slightly. It was a difference in the atmosphere that struck me: hereabouts lived those upon whom the Soviet smiled and rewarded – the *apparatchiks*, the Party leaders and full-time Party officials, also to a lesser extent the doctors, the teachers, the engineers, the writers, the latter just so long as they wrote what the leadership required. Olga Menshikova hadn't told me what Katrina's profession was, or even whether she was married in which case her status would be due to her husband rather than herself. In fact, apart from the code name, I was entirely in the dark. I was also far from unaware of the risks inherent in approaching unknown persons in Moscow; but there had been something about Olga Menshikova that made me trust her. Part of that something was her concern for old man Melensky, retainer of the Menshikovs of yore. So that when we reached Katrina's block and had climbed by the stairs, not trusting the shaky-looking lift, and had knocked at the door on the eighth floor, and this had been quickly opened, and loud music had come out, I was not unduly worried. The woman who opened the door fitted the given description. She was tall and angular, long thin nose, large spectacles, flat chest, narrow hips and an austere expression. I put her down as possibly a teacher.

I asked, "Katrina?"

The response was in Russian. "Who enquires?"

122

I answered indirectly. I said, "I come from a friend, west of Moscow. A lady." I hesitated. "Where the birds sing." This was the password given me by Olga Menshikova. The door came wider open and we were invited in. The radio stayed on, drowning bugs. We went into a narrow passage off which three doors opened. There was no carpet in the passage, just bare concrete. Even the smiled-upon were not accorded luxury; only the politicals got that, and the military.

"You are not Russian," Katrina said flatly.

"No."

"You are from London?" She was speaking English now, heavily accented.

"Yes," I said. Then I asked, "How much do you know?"

"Enough for me to understand. I shall not ask your name but I shall ask some questions. Please come in and sit down."

She opened the nearer door and went through. We followed; the austerity was everywhere. Here there was a thin carpet but little else. A hard-looking sofa and two barely upholstered chairs not to be described as easy, a polished table, a bookcase filled with what seemed to be learned works, an electric fire the single bar of which gave little heat, though the contrast with the outside air was welcome enough. Over this fire, set beneath an ornament-bare shelf doing duty as a mantelpiece, was a large photograph of Comrade Gorbachev. All very stark, like Katrina herself. I put her down as unmarried; certainly there was no ring and she had the look of someone to whom sex was anathema. The hips were scarcely child-bearing ones.

"The questions?" I said as Felicity and I sat on the hard-looking chairs. Katrina remained standing, staring down at us.

"The telling. By you."

"Of what?"

"Of all, please. From the start. You may trust me."

Because of Olga Menshikova I thought I could. In any

123

case, I had little option and I believed that Katrina held the key that I needed. So, with reservations, of course, about 6D2 and Whitehall, I told her the lot, right up to the train lift into Moscow. The advent of Storvac following upon the abortive border crossing near Braunlage in West Germany, the journey to Minsk, the crucifixion, the arrival of Comrade Grulke after the marsh interment, the sojourn with the ESP and the drugs – just as I had told Olga Menshikova. She listened intently and when I had finished she remained deep in thought, still standing, looking not at us now but out of the window at the continuing snowfall and the iron-hard sky tinged ominously with red as it lowered itself onto the Kremlin towers. I broke into her thoughts.

"Olga Menshikova," I said.

"Yes?"

"She's a communist, genuinely?"

"She is a communist, yes. Convincedly. A patriot."

"In spite of her background?"

"Perhaps because of it. Naturally, one of her age does not herself remember the old days. But although she never took part in the terror and slavery on the one hand, the arrogance and the luxury on the other, she is aware of history as we all are. Do you understand, Comrade?"

I said, "Yes, I think I do. She's ashamed of her background?"

"Certain aspects of it only – yes. And she wishes to make amends. But not in the way that Greenfly does. Comrade Menshikova, I say again, is a patriot, and does not wish to see the Soviets at war, in which so many citizens will die and there will be so much destruction."

Olga Menshikova had herself said something similar. I was about to probe further when Katrina lifted a hand to stop me. She said, "There was news on the radio this morning. Bodies were found by the railway line. These will be the ones you have told me of."

"Yes," I said, and waited for her to go on. I felt in my

inside pocket for the wallet and the letter I had taken from the dead man. I meant to read them in privacy, even though I trusted Katrina. It's never a bad idea to have some knowledge kept to oneself whatever the trust, when you're right out on a limb in a land like Russia. That was, if any knowledge lay in the letter.

Katrina said, "That was all, the bare statement."

"No prognostications?"

"None."

"But the authorities will be looking for – someone."

"Yes. You must conceal yourselves until it is safe for you to start your journey back to London."

I felt a surge of blood. I said, "With the required information. The information the Ladybirds wished to pass but couldn't. What is it, Comrade Katrina?"

"I shall show you. Then you must leave here – I shall tell you where it is safe to go. First, you look hungry."

I saw the look of sheer relief on Felicity's face and I said, "We are, very – "

"I shall prepare food. It will not take long." She left the room and I heard her footsteps on the concrete floor of the passage and the opening of a door. I brought out the wallet and letter. I opened the wallet first: the usual clutter, some rouble notes, an identity card – not KGB – what looked like a personal letter in scratchy writing, photographs of what could be a wife and two children, a reminder to me of the tragedy that came from intrigue, espionage and undercover activity generally, a widow and orphans to mourn a breadwinner. Then I came upon other things in the back compartment of the wallet: more photographs, this time pornographic. All sorts of poses and acts, some of them in close-up. It was lucky for the dead man's reputation that I'd nicked them before they landed up with his effects in his wife's hands.

The wallet was useless: I tried the envelope quickly, before Katrina came back into the room. The contents were brief and to the point, a single typed sheet of paper,

125

official paper bearing the insignia of the Soviet Defence Ministry and containing orders. Simple, direct orders: an Englishman and an Englishwoman were known to be inside Russia. The names were given: Shaw and Mandrake, which made us look like a firm of estate agents or solicitors. We were to be apprehended, alive if possible. The 'if possible', I knew, didn't mean a lot. I dare say something showed in my face; Felicity asked what was in the envelope. I didn't want to say it was our death warrant, signed, sealed and delivered. I shrugged, and said it was official bumph, but she wasn't deceived.

"It's more than that," she said.

"All right, it is. But I'm not too worried." That was true; I wasn't, basically. It was only to be expected. We had both known the risks all along. It was just that it had been a shade startling to see it in cold type . . .

Katrina came back with food. Timewise the hour was half way between breakfast and lunch; the food was coarse, and it was cold. Some tough meat, cold sliced potatoes, the ubiquitous black bread, but we wolfed it down. Katrina brought coffee, rather acorn-like but very welcome and we lit cigarettes after asking permission. Katrina gave it but didn't seem to like it much; ostentatiously she waved smoke away with her hand, a large and bony one.

I decided, after all, to show her the letter, or warrant.

She read it, not seeming surprised. She said, "Shaw and Mandrake, that is you. I know the signature. Comrade Vasyutin."

"Yes?" I said.

"Vasyutin is a member of Greenfly. This is official only to Greenfly. Not to the Supreme Soviet."

I was puzzled and said so. Katrina said Greenfly had members in all the Ministries and inside the seats of power in the Kremlin, men who were believed by the Soviet leadership to be straightforward members of the officially-approved WUSWIPP. That they were members of WUS-WIPP was true, but Greenfly were a break-away group within WUSWIPP.

126

"I know that," I said. "But – "

"The time has come to tell you the facts," Katrina said.

It was a strange story and a gripping one. Put very shortly, the Soviet Union was about to mount a pre-emptive strike against the West. No warning; the missiles were set to go. Great Britain would be attacked and so would West Germany, with the Russian and East German armoured divisions ready to cross the frontier all the way along as soon as it was safe fall-out-wise to do so. BAOR would be decimated, Bonn, Paris, and the other NATO capitals made untenable. The Soviet nuclear-powered and missile-armed submarines off the American coast would mount their attacks on Washington and New York.

I asked exactly when this was to happen.

Katrina didn't know but repeated her belief that it was imminent. She said the official Soviet leadership didn't want it to happen, that they were fighting what had turned into a rearguard action against those of their number who did want it to happen.

"Greenfly?" I asked.

"Yes. Greenfly wishes to use the know-how of WUS-WIPP to bring to an end the East-West conflict, to settle it for all time. But the leadership in the Kremlin knows very well that the West will not be easily subdued and that Russia will suffer – as I have said. Nevertheless, when Greenfly wins, the strike will commence."

"You think they will win?"

Katrina was positive. She said, "Yes, they will win. It is a question of time only."

"And I'm expected to stop it?" I asked rather sourly, seeing myself as an unlikely preventer of war all on my own.

"No. To take the facts to your country, to your Prime Minister. That was what one of our Ladybirds was attempting to do when – "

"Yes," I said. "I know that. Why hasn't it been possible

to get the word through long before now? Why wait for me?"

She gave a bitter smile. "You do not know the Soviets! All the time everyone is watched, I for one – "

"We'll have been reported as visiting you, then."

"There is always the risk, yes, but some risks have to be taken or there is no progress at all – you must know this – "

"Yes," I said. "I do know. And you? You're prepared to – "

"I am prepared to give my life. I am not afraid." The tall, thin body seemed to grow taller as Katrina loomed over me like an animated skeleton. "The individual is lesser than the cause. The Soviets have made great strides, have made many achievements since the Revolution. These must not be jeopardised by the wild men of Greenfly . . ." She went off into quite a tirade: here was one hundred percent dedication and fanaticism. I caught Felicity's eye: she seemed fascinated by the performance, which came to an end after about a couple of concentrated minutes.

When Katrina had run out of steam I asked her again why it had not been possible to get word through to the West, and what it was thought the West would do when the word did get through. I asked, "What about our Embassy?"

She said, "Your Radley-Bewick."

"Now dead. I told you."

"Yes. He was our contact, as of course you know – "

"Yes, I – "

"He had not passed anything on to the British Embassy."

"No," I said. "I knew that too." Arthur Webb in Focal House had said that even Radley-Bewick hadn't been told the facts, and now I asked why this was, and got the answer I'd been given when I'd asked Webb the same question: the Ladybirds wouldn't take a chance with Radley-Bewick, who was closely watched by the KGB.

"And Greenfly?" I asked.

128

"Yes."

"But surely," I said in much bewilderment, "something would have leaked through to our Embassy? They have their intelligence services, after all! They're not asleep the whole time. This is exactly the sort of situation they're supposed to monitor."

She shrugged. "It has been very secret, so secret that – "

"But *you* know," I pointed out.

"Yes, we know. We also have our people, our women, in high places. One of our number has been party to all that has gone on within Greenfly. It is she who has warned the official Party leadership and the Supreme Soviet. As a result there has been the most iron-hard fist on all possible dissemination of intelligence and information generally. The Kremlin has no wish for the West to learn the facts, Comrade Shaw – "

"In case the West goes moving as to war," I murmured more or less to myself, and Katrina nodded. "An interesting situation," I went on. "Just me and Comrade Mandrake, to prevent the total nuclearisation of the northern hemisphere!"

"Yes," Katrina said. "But I have not yet told you all there is to tell."

There was something very ominous in her tone and her eyes had taken on an inward look. I said, "Then you'd better get on with it, Comrade. If you're being watched – "

"Yes," she said again. "I have not told you how and where the strike is to be made – that is, the first strike of all, before the saturation attack is mounted by the Soviet missiles and the armoured divisions."

"The *first* strike?"

"This will come from one of your British missile-armed submarines, Comrade Shaw."

I laughed, but without any humour. She was being ridiculous. I said, "The British, pre-empting the pre-emptive Russian strike? Somehow I can't see that being authorised by my government unless the message has got through. Which currently it hasn't. Even if it had, I don't believe we'd mount the first attack." This was true: my view was that once that message of approaching doom reached London, Whitehall would blow the whole thing sky-high by getting on the hot line to the Kremlin and revealing their knowledge. With the Greenfly guns spiked in advance, the official Soviet line would be re-established and we would all stagger on together towards the Armageddon that might come in time but which would have been delayed a few more years, a few more years' breathing space for the world's warriors either to go on beating the drum or really try for peace. Once again, I thought, it all came down to a question of time; and I wanted to be on my way out of Russia, fast, a jump or two ahead of my potential liquidators. I said as much to Katrina.

This time it was she who laughed and I didn't like the implications. Then she came out with it: the first missile, to be fired from a British nuclear-powered submarine on patrol off the Bay of Biscay, would land harmlessly – more or less – in a sparsely populated part of the enormous Soviet land mass, up north along the fringe of the Kara Sea. That would start the ball rolling. I asked her in amazement how she knew this and whether she thought the British Prime Minister had gone mad. She didn't go into details as to how she knew – obviously, in view of her next bombshell, it was another Ladybird contact inside the Greenfly set-up – but she said, and this was the bombshell, that the British Prime Minister wouldn't know anything about it, nor would the Ministry of Defence in Whitehall. The missile would be activated by electronic beams, an interference with the weapons' system by the clever boys in Russia, the Greenfly faction using the WUSWIPP know-how. Even Greenfly liked to be shown as whiter than white before the courts of international public opinion and who could blame the Soviets when Britain fired the first shot without provocation?

My mind was going round in circles, filled with racing

thoughts of a nuclear holocaust with Britain as the bad boy – I didn't doubt WUSWIPP could have come up with something technical like this, didn't doubt it for a moment – and I failed to hear something else the Ladybird said. I asked for a repeat. She said very distinctly, "There will be assistance from thoughts thrown onto a screen."

I jerked back to Katrina's presence. "You can't mean the ESP stuff?"

She nodded. "A defector from your country – known to Radley-Bewick, which is one reason why Radley-Bewick could not be wholly trusted." She gave me the defector's name: it was known to me as that of a scientist from the Ministry of Defence, not, I would have thought, an important man but certainly one of some useful knowledge and his defection, not long before in fact, had caused a rumpus in the press. Katrina said this man had personal knowledge of the British missile-firing submarine fleet and had been many times to sea on exercises. His drug-induced thoughts, if dead Senyavin's process worked without the presence of the mastermind – but there would be other Senyavins who would have been trained up to its use – that man's thoughts and know-how might very well be a handy adjunct to electronic interference, almost a text-book guide to effective procedure.

I asked, "Tell me, Comrade: do you believe in all this? The ESP business?"

She said it wasn't quite ESP as the experts knew it but yes, she did. I thought she looked the sort of person who might. Those dark deep-set eyes and the intensity. She said Comrade Mandrake and I must now go, and make our way out of Russia. In heartfelt fashion I agreed. She gave me a name and an address, a friend of Radley-Bewick who would make certain arrangements, one who did not know the facts but knew that Radley-Bewick wanted to make contact with a western agent. This person could be trusted, she said.

I had just mentioned the documentary proof referred to

131

by Olga Menshikova when heavy banging came at Katrina's front door and echoed like the knell of doom along the concrete passage. Katrina went very white and began shaking, a hand to her mouth. I said, "Hold on a moment – "

"They will break down the door!"

"Yes," I said. "That's why I want a moment to re-assemble the guns."

11

Felicity and I were ready with the assembled guns as Katrina opened the door. I heard her say something, then she was cut off by a man's voice and there was a brief scuffle and a short, sharp cry. A few moments later, by which time we'd concealed ourselves behind the open door of the sitting-room, I heard the footsteps coming along the concrete. No-one entered the room: I hadn't really expected the visitors to be fooled by an apparently empty room, but it had been the only thing I could do.

A man's voice spoke again. "We know you are there. You were seen to enter."

I kept silent; Felicity's breathing hit my ears like a drum. The voice said, "I will count to ten. Then I will kill the woman, the Ladybird."

Somehow it didn't sound like the KGB. They kill, but in private, and they aren't normally so blatant about it. I settled for Greenfly. I wasn't going to contribute to Katrina's death so I gave Felicity a nudge and we both came out, holding the machine-pistols. I saw a short man, thick-set, with shoulders like a bison, and only one eye. The left one was just a black, wrinkled socket. He was accompanied by another man, a younger one with a foxy face and a ginger moustache. It was this man who was holding Katrina and twisting both her arms up behind her back. She looked agonised, her eyes staring and mouth trembling.

The thick-set man said, "So. It *is* you. Shaw and Mandrake."

"What makes you think so?"

"I have your descriptions." He spoke good English. "You have now reached the end of the road, my friends."

"I doubt it," I said coolly, though I knew he could be right.

"The guns. Place them on the floor, with the butts towards me."

"Why should we?"

The man grinned. "Because if you do not, the woman dies."

"You won't risk gunfire in a block of flats."

"It has been done before. In Moscow, one does not interfere – it is never wise to interfere. In any case, death does not come always by guns alone." As he'd been speaking he'd been sliding a hand into the front of his jacket and now it reappeared holding a thin, fairly long knife, a very nasty job with a tapering point. "You understand now?"

I nodded. "I understand," I said. Meekly, I bent to lay my gun on the floor. I fancied the Russian was a shade too confident: that happens to people who live under dictatorships and who are part of the élite, the upper crust of intellectuals and scientists, and this one, in spite of his build and general demeanour, didn't strike me as being the action-man type with fast reflexes. I proved right. He didn't react half fast enough when I came suddenly out of my bent position and slammed the barrel of the gun into his mouth so hard that I think it went right through the roof and left him speechless and staggering. Blood poured and the knife clattered down to the thin carpet. Felicity picked it up, looking white, and handed it to me. I said, "Hang onto it for now." I had the second man covered. He was looking as if he wanted to be far, far away, all fight gone.

I said, "Let go of the lady," and he did so. Katrina went shakily across to a chair and sat. Outside, the day was still dark with the falling snow. The thick-set man was

134

lying in a heap on the floor, making moaning sounds. I didn't know the prognosis for a shattered mouth-roof but he looked as though he was bleeding to death and if the barrel had gone far enough I reckoned that his brain might never be the same again. I kept the ginger moustache covered and asked its wearer for identification and explanation.

It was Katrina who answered. "They are Greenfly," she said.

"I thought as much. You know them?"

"Yes." She gave me their names but they didn't convey anything to me. They wouldn't be the big boys of the WUSWIPP break-away faction; the brass wouldn't take any personal risks in public. "They are here for – what you spoke of."

The documentation, the proof to be taken back to London before it was too late. But I didn't want to go into that just then. I didn't want Katrina to say she had it in the flat. And I was, in fact, wondering what to do next. The thick-set man might die if left – I just didn't know. The other man was very much alive. I could not, of course, let them go. I couldn't leave them, either. Katrina could come with us to find Radley-Bewick's friend and I would keep her safe to the best of my ability, taking her back to London if possible to tell her own story in Whitehall. But to leave the two Russians behind would ensure that we never did get back to England, any of us – or anyway, at the very least it would make the whole thing that much more hazardous. But I didn't like the idea of killing in cold blood, killing men who were now defenceless. To say nothing of the noise. I wasn't entirely convinced by the thick-set man's statement that in Moscow one didn't interfere. But I could use the knife.

As matters turned out, my conscience was allowed to remain intact.

*

It was a flat of death now, death and a lot of blood and general mess. Felicity and I left at speed after we had made a thorough search of the whole place, looking for that documentation. Unsuccessfully – it just was not there, neither was it on Katrina's now dead person. Either Olga Menshikova had had her facts wrong or Katrina had decided it was too dangerous to keep and had passed it on. If so, God alone knew where to. Radley-Bewick's friend? Maybe.

"Nasty," I said to Felicity as we reached the street hoping we weren't under observation – there didn't seem to be anyone around; the weather was thick and quite appalling and keeping obbo today wouldn't be anyone's idea of a policeman's happy lot, though the thought of Siberia could be presumed to keep all hands on the ball.

Felicity shivered, not, I thought, with the cold alone. It had been slaughter and Katrina had started it – very bravely. She had said earlier that she would die for the cause, the cause basically of peace. It could be that the Ladybirds were in their own way the Soviet's equivalent of our Peace Women, though there had been nothing peaceful about Katrina when she had got suddenly up from her chair. She had become a wildcat, unstoppable as she flung herself on Felicity and wrested the knife away and turned viciously on the younger man, who hadn't a chance, being unarmed and taken, as we all were, by surprise. The knife had gone through his throat and he had gasped himself to death, drowning in his own welling blood. I dropped my gun and grabbed her but her elbow, a sharp and bony one, was slammed backwards into my face and I tripped over the other body and fell; it had been ignominious and it had given Katrina time to use the knife on the thick-set Greenfly – the throat again. By this time Felicity was covering her with the other gun, too late of course and with not much purpose left since we could assume Katrina wouldn't attack her allies, though she looked crazy enough just then to do anything.

136

A second later I realised she wasn't well, physically. Her face had gone deathly white and her breathing had become stertorous. Then she collapsed in a heap, with her face all twisted up, the mouth awry, tugged down at one corner.

"I think she's had a stroke," Felicity said. "Or a heart attack."

I bent down by her side. No heart beat, and the eyes, still open, glazed over. I could detect no breath and I got on my feet again. "Dead," I said. That was when we made the search, and then got out, closing the front door behind us so that it locked on the Russian equivalent of a Yale.

All dead, and no noise. That, at any rate, was something. Plus our intact consciences.

We went back, struggled back, through the snow, across Moscow, past the Kremlin again. I was not too worried about the lack of documentation: I reckoned I had enough weight inside 6D2 to make my story stick and be acted upon. And did I believe it all? The answer was yes, I did. So many lives had been and were being risked, and I knew WUSWIPP of old. They were a brilliant bunch of bastards, and I mean bastards even if this time they were acting in the cause of peace against Greenfly. It was the WUSWIPP know-how behind it all and I had no reason whatever to doubt that they could do the job – or rather that Greenfly could do it. Underwater interference by radio impulses, beams and so on, would not have been possible when last I had been familiar with submarines but times had changed and WUSWIPP could always be relied upon to find a way and the ship's company of whichever nuclear sub it was wouldn't have a chance to correct, negative or abort. At least, that would be the theory. It just might not work out in practice but that couldn't be banked on: Greenfly would have done their homework and made plenty of tests and dummy runs.

My mind going off at a tangent I said, "I wish I'd asked

137

Katrina about the crucifixion angle. There must be a reason."

"Just anti-Christ," Felicity suggested.

"Symbolic?"

"Could be."

We trudged on, muffled in our padded anoraks, hands deep in pockets. We still had the guns: somehow by this time I hadn't wanted to part with them. The traffic was virtually non-existent now, for some reason or other, and I found it alarming, only military transport seemed to be moving, with chained tyres or caterpillar tracks, and the pedestrians were few. That made us stand out and we kept away from the big squares and the main thoroughfares. I was certain we had no tail but I didn't like the atmosphere. I wondered how often the military was so evident in the Moscow streets. Maybe it was just my personal knowledge of what was scheduled to happen; maybe it wasn't. Time could be shortening rather fast for comfort, the men in the Kremlin being pushed by Greenfly to the final act – that was the feeling that gripped me, anyway, a feeling of doom that was not going to be averted. As if sensing the way I was thinking, Felicity asked what action could be taken by Whitehall if ever we made it back across the border.

I gave her my earlier thoughts, that the hot line to the Kremlin would be used to spike the guns. I said, "In the meantime, Defence Ministry will bring in all the missile fleet from patrol and disarm them."

"If there's time."

"Yes," I said, and left it at that. In all probability there wouldn't be time. Greenfly might go into action the moment they got word I was over the frontier, or even before, stymying the official Soviet leadership, forcing them into action, making their interference signals before Whitehall could react. Even if Whitehall didn't use the hot line right away but brought in the subs first, any sudden deviation from patrol would be noted by the Greenfly monitors and interpreted aright, and the first strike would

138

be sent off to start World War Three. There would never be a World War Four once the nuclear clouds drifted across the northern half of the globe. Armageddon, just as the Bible had predicted. Was there some link with that dreadful crucifixion of Yasnov's daughter in Minsk? The symbol of the saving of sinners, to be cruelly and blasphemously followed by the triumph of the devil and the extermination of half the world?

I was growing fanciful. I thrust it out of my mind. We moved on unhindered. In the side streets we lost the military movements and there were more people around, housewives at their shopping, lifting booted feet above the snow, their faces frozen beneath the fur caps on their heads, so many of them looking old and pinched, probably old beyond their actual years. Moscow was a hard place to live in, especially in winter.

It was a little over an hour's walk from Katrina's flat to the flat of Radley-Bewick's friend. The name Katrina had given me was Comrade Sharef. A Jew. The Soviet didn't like Jews and there was good reason for Jews not to like the Soviet. Comrade Sharef lived in a block of flats as had Katrina but it was a tenement block for workers without that extra comfort accorded the élite, and it was forbidding and dirty and seemed to be filled with hordes of children tearing around the concrete passages and staircases, intent on some game or other.

We grinned matily as we were almost knocked flat by half-a-dozen juveniles moving at speed. It wouldn't do to take up British attitudes. Or what had once been British attitudes of discipline.

"Little buggers," I muttered to Felicity. The noise was appalling and I might just as well have shouted. We went up seven floors and knocked at Comrade Sharef's door. The door was quickly opened by a woman, or what looked like a woman, a very over-painted one with a suggestion of hairs on her arms and the look of a razor having been used. I remembered that at no time had Katrina mentioned

Comrade Sharef's sex and had in fact used the term 'person'. Now I understood why: Comrade Sharef was a transvestite.

"Who are you?" The voice, speaking Russian as would be expected, could have been of either sex.

I said, "We come from where the birds sing." Sharef nodded and gestured us to enter, standing aside to let us through. The place stank; there was no other word. Comrade Sharef was using a violent scent and at the end of the passage was a pile of garbage, old bits of food wrapped in copies of *Pravda*. Dust lay thick everywhere and as Comrade Sharef moved and stirred the air there was indication, right through the scent, that he didn't wash as often as he might.

What, I wondered, had come over Radley-Bewick since he'd left Britain? Comrade Sharef by no means went with Eton and Christ Church; but possibly he had hidden attractions, though I would never have thought it of Radley-Bewick.

In Russian, I asked, "Do you speak English, Comrade?"

He did; he'd learned the language from his friend, he said.

"Radley-Bewick?"

"Yes. How do I trust you, Comrade?"

I said, "I don't know how you do, but I promise you you can. Naturally I carry no identification, but I come from Olga Menshikova and Katrina. Before that, Comrade Storvac. And Comrade Yasnov."

It was quite a list of trustworthy names and Sharef nodded at each like a massive bird pecking corn – he, or she, was in fact a massive man, or woman, with a long nose and a wide, sensual mouth. There was a tendency to middle-aged spread and no breasts, not surprisingly if I was right about the sex. We were ushered into a room not unlike Katrina's but smaller and less well furnished: no books and no sofa and an even thinner carpet. We were left to stand while Sharef sat with his legs apart and his

140

skirt lifted to just below his knees, not the way normal to a lady, and I caught a glimpse of what looked like calico knickers and muscular thighs.

"What do you want?" he asked.

I said, "I come from London. I come for a message. Now I have the message. I wish to return to London. It is vital that I do so quickly. I understand that you're aware your friend wanted to contact . . . someone from the West. Perhaps you know also that Radley-Bewick is dead."

I was unprepared for Comrade Sharef to burst into tears but that is what he did. Between sobs and cries he said yes, he did know. Only an hour or so earlier he had had a message from a trustworthy source. Only now, he sobbed, was he beginning to take it in. Was it really true? I said yes it was. I had seen no sign of tears up to now: I supposed he'd been in a state of limbo and what I said had breached the dam. He wept and wept, twisting his body about on the hard chair. I didn't know how to comfort him and time was passing. His agitation was wafting the scent about and I felt suffocated. Felicity was waving a handkerchief in front of her nose. Comrade Sharef, if he noticed, didn't seem offended.

I said, "Come now, Comrade. You must do your best for your friend now he is gone. You must pull yourself together and listen, and you must help. For Radley-Bewick's sake." I wished I could recall Radley-Bewick's christian name but I couldn't, and bare Radley-Bewick, in a moment of stress and mourning, sounded heartless. I looked at Felicity for some feminine help, but she shook her head and grimaced and I got the message: it wasn't feminine sympathy Comrade Sharef wanted, nor the gentle touch of a girlish hand. But I wasn't cut out for the other role.

I sharpened my voice. "Listen," I said, and he stared back at me big-eyed, mouth open. "We need help. Katrina said you would help." I refrained from mentioning another death just then, even that of a woman. "Katrina said you

141

would help us to get out of Russia, and back to London –
with the message your friend wanted passed. Can you do
this, Comrade Sharef?"

He began to pull himself together. A compact came out
and fresh rouge was applied to the tear-induced runnels;
another compact produced powder. The effect was dreadful
but the action appeared calming: a new face was always a
help, I supposed. Soon he might go out and buy a new
hat. Anyway, he said he could probably help, though it
would be an immense risk for him as well as for ourselves.
Like Katrina he was willing to take the risk; he had loved
Radley-Bewick. He said so.

"A kind man and a sad one," he said, sniffing.

Comrade Sharef, I thought, looked far from a happy
man himself. Exiles and homosexuals, there was an affinity
in sadness. But Radley-Bewick had been no ordinary exiled
traitor; he had been a plant and never a traitor. There had
always been that chance he would return to Britain, if not
in overt honour then certainly in good odour with the
Establishment. He might never have been given a knight-
hood but he would have lived out his life in comfort once
his usefulness inside Russia had come to an end and an
exchange had been effected.

I quizzed Comrade Sharef about Radley-Bewick. Why, I
asked, had it been impossible for Radley-Bewick, even if
he didn't know the nature of the threat, at least to warn
the West that there was something in the air? That, more
or less, had been supposed to be his function. But Sharef
couldn't answer that one; I was left to assume that the very
fact Radley-Bewick had passed word that a woman was
coming through the East German wire was in itself not
only enough in his view but literally all he had been in a
position to pass. Again, the non-sharing of knowledge, the
close secrecy because the eye of Greenfly was everywhere.
And the ear: like Katrina, Comrade Sharef had switched
his radio on full blast. In Russia, you didn't trust your life
to a simple bug search.

142

I said, "Well, the sooner we start the better. Have you a route, and safe houses?"

"I know of persons, yes. Myself I do not come with you."

I nodded: just as well really. Comrade Sharef would attract attention. Then he corrected himself: he would come a little way, to where we would contact the person who, as he put it, commanded the route out, the one with the contacts, the safe houses.

I made a guess. "Ladybirds?"

"Yes."

"Can you not give me directions?"

He could not. "It is not safe – you will see. The address must not be spoken to anyone."

"In case of – accidents?"

"That, perhaps – if you were taken and interrogated. But you will see."

That was all he would say. I wondered why it was all right for *him* to know the address: he didn't look to me the sort who would stand up for long under KGB violence, or Greenfly violence or whatever. But, of course, you never could tell. He could be as tough as old boots and never mind the recent tears. After that Comrade Sharef didn't waste time. He got to his feet and pulled on a big, heavy cloak with a hood. We left the flat and went out into the freezing cold. Snowflakes dappled Comrade Sharef's hood, from which stray ends of peroxided blonde hair peeped and straggled. The cloak covered his more outrageous aspects; he lost his attention-attracting flamboyance and I was much relieved. We moved anonymously through the snow, just three more Muscovites braving the weather to go shopping, a man, perhaps, with his wife and mother-in-law. Up to a point we did go shopping: Comrade Sharef entered a baker's, gesturing us to follow him in. From the women, two of them, behind the counter he asked for a loaf.

"For my friends, good friends."

I was aware of the women watching me and Felicity closely. One of them said something *sotte voce* to Comrade Sharef, who nodded in reply. The woman who had spoken lifted a flap in the counter and Sharef went through, again gesturing us to follow. There was the unnerving feeling of a trap, but we were committed now. We needed Comrade Sharef and I had no reason for mistrust, but I kept a hand ready for the heavy part of the stripped-down gun.

12

We went into a small back room lit only by a candle in a
bottle which Comrade Sharef had picked up and ignited
whilst on the way through a long, narrow passage. The
flame guttered and flickered eerily off dirty walls with
peeling paper and a smell of long established damp. Not a
word was said. Once in the room, Sharef reached out for a
bell-pull set in the wall beside another door and gave it a
jerk.

Very distantly, I heard a bell tinkle. After that there was
a long wait. I asked Sharef if he wasn't worried that we
might have been tailed. He wasn't. A tail there might have
been – though in fact I hadn't noted one – but we certainly
wouldn't be followed in here, either by the KGB or
Greenfly. His tone said he didn't wish to be questioned
further. I was left to make the large assumption that the
women in the shop were Ladybirds. (Later, I discovered I
was wrong in that.) As we waited impatiently and in my
case anyway with a stomach-loosening sensation of extreme
danger, I thought backwards with time on my mind. It
was almost unbelievable that a mere four days earlier –
always assuming I hadn't been in drug-induced sleep for
longer than I believed in the Greenfly establishment with
the doctor and Senyavin – four days ago we had been in
the West, in Braunlage. Time was playing tricks. And
time was currently passing slowly; but at last there came
some sort of response to that bell.

There was a click, that was all, and the door ahead of us
came slightly open. Comrade Sharef gave it a push.

"Follow," he said. He had thrown back his hood now and the blond hair streamed in the candlelight. The cloak now gave him the appearance of a mad bat. With the candle held high, he walked along another passage, one that seemed to take a gentle downhill slope. Seen from behind, Comrade Sharef on the move was quite a sight: he had the build of a man who would stride right out, really long steps, but he didn't, he minced with little short steps and although the cloak hid his bottom I could imagine the buttock movements, up and down.

We walked for a long way, still in the pervading smell of damp. Also drains; it was horrible and stifling but I had to assume it was leading ultimately to the West. The surface of what had all the attributes of a subterranean tunnel was uneven and we stumbled about a bit from time to time. Not Comrade Sharef who had obviously been this way before and knew all the pitfalls. Wondering where the tunnel might end got me nowhere: I would find out soon enough.

I did.

Sharef halted by another door, not in fact at the end of the tunnel but set into the wall on our right. He turned round and said, "When we are admitted, you will wait – I shall show you. I shall then leave you. Another person will come. You will be in good hands. You will of course remain very, very quiet."

I said we would, not half. I said, inadequately, "Thank you for your help. I hope you won't suffer as a result, Comrade."

"If you remain quiet, then I shall not."

He reached out and knocked on the door, not loudly, three times followed by a pause, then two more knocks. We had another wait and then the door opened, cautiously at first. There was some talk in Russian and we were admitted by a young woman who placed a finger across her lips. She shut the tunnel door. We were in dim light from an electric bulb high overhead, and I heard distant music, the strumming of a guitar I fancied, rather haunting. Like Comrade Sharef himself, the place smelled of scent. It didn't take me long to guess that we had arrived in a brothel. I knew that in Russia brothels didn't exist and prostitution was a crime, but this applied in the main to the masses. The élite was treated differently. They wouldn't call it a brothel, of course; but it would be used for that purpose by the high-up Party officials, the bureaucrats and the military.

The young woman showed us into a room little bigger than a cupboard leading off the sleazy lobby.

"You will wait," she said in English – whispered the words into my ear. "I shall not be long, Comrade." Sharef was already mincing away through another door and going, I guessed, to do his duty: not all the élite, the men who came and went by devious means through the tunnel via the baker's shop – which would have been why Sharef had been so certain the KGB wouldn't follow – not all would have normal sexual desires and Comrade Sharef was there to fulfil a need. Also perhaps to fulfill another need, the need for people from the West sometimes to be compromised? Photographs from hidden cameras, and then the blackmail? I shuddered at the thought of being compromised with Comrade Sharef. But, for his present purposes as an ally of the Ladybirds, it was all pretty good cover.

I hoped it was, anyway. Right now we were firmly in Sharef's hands. But in our situation you had to trust someone. Without help we could never hope to make our way out of Russia. That was an axiom.

Obeying orders, we kept silent. Bugs might be found even in what seemed to be a broom cupboard. That cupboard acted as a sort of sound box in the other direction, though: we heard voices, men and women, laughter, giggles, other sounds. Now, and then, more distantly, the music again and song. No doubt, officially, the brothel was simply a place of music and vodka, a relaxation for the

147

brass, what in the West we would call a drinking club. I wished we could see just who patronised it. While we waited in thick darkness, other knocks came at the tunnel door and were answered and we heard the young woman's welcoming voice as the clientele entered and clumped through to their pleasures. In a short while I counted fourteen: someone would be having a busy time.

The young woman opened the door at last: it had felt like years. But she hadn't come to release us. She put her lips close to my ear and whispered, "You will wait longer, please. There has been a delay."

"What sort of delay?"

"The car. Also it will be safer to wait until the early hours when no new clients come and those that are here are drunk."

Or safe in bed, I thought. But I saw the girl's point. Before I could say anything she went on, "The car will now come at two o'clock in the morning. When it is here, I will come. I am sorry for the delay." She went away. I was sorry too: I was growing desperate in that wretched cupboard, a case of creeping claustrophobia. I couldn't do anything other than hold Felicity close, so small was the space, but now I held her even closer and tried to give her comfort and reassurance. In fact she was doing very well so far but the thought of all those extra hours in darkness and constriction wasn't funny – and the need for total silence made it worse. Imagination ran riot: Comrade Sharef had done the dirty on us and shopped us to the KGB . . . but if he'd done that, then they wouldn't be wasting time, they would have come for us right away. I forced down thoughts of treachery: Sharef hadn't seemed like that and the tears for dead Radley-Bewick had been genuine, and we were friends of Radley-Bewick's, well vouched for by Olga Menshikova and Katrina, neither of whom would as it were have onforwarded us to him if we were not on the level. So if Comrade Sharef shopped us he would shop himself as well.

Logical: but it didn't entirely suppress uneasy thoughts and that long wait loomed like eternity. Every footstep, every voice outside, brought the sweat pouring. I didn't even dare to drop off though once or twice I found it hard to keep my eyelids apart – the close atmosphere was having its effect. If I dropped off I might snore.

The door opened, very quietly. So quietly that I wasn't aware of it until slightly fresher air came in. The lobby was totally dark. I felt a light touch on my shoulder, a girl's hand.

"Come," she said.

"The car . . . ?"

"At the end of the tunnel."

We came out, stiff and weary. I stretched my limbs, took Felicity's hand. It felt cold and she was shaking. I reckoned we'd been let out just about in time. The Russian girl took my other hand and pulled and I heard the outer door opening. We followed through into the tunnel. When she had closed the door behind us she fumbled about and struck a match with which she lit a candle. Ghostly light flickered and things scuttled away around our feet, rats, mice, I didn't know. The light didn't reach the floor. But it showed me the strain in Felicity's face and I was glad when our guide, who had to be a Ladybird, said in an encouraging voice, "Now it will not be long. We go not to the baker's shop but the other direction where the car waits."

"With a driver?" I asked.

"Yes."

"One of the Ladybirds? Or a man?"

"A Ladybird," she answered. We were moving now, and to move felt good, even in the foul-smelling tunnel. "The car will take you out of Moscow and will drive all

149

day. In the evening you will reach a safe house and will change cars for the next stage. It is all arranged."

I asked where we were to cross into the West. I asked what the cover would be. She was non-committal about the cover, but she said we would be driven south-west to the three-way frontier town of Chop on the Soviet-Hungary-Czechoslovakia borders and thence into Austria via St Gotthard. Detailed instructions would reach me en route, and the cars would be driven fast. The girl knew the urgency.

This end of the tunnel was shorter than the way we'd come with Sharef. After only a few minutes' stumbling walk in the candlelight, up slightly rising ground, we saw a heavy door ahead. The girl used a key and opened it. At first the darkness was thick but as bitter cold struck through I saw the loom of snow: we had emerged into the open. So far as I could see the surroundings had the look of something like a builder's yard, with snow-covered ladders lying stacked, and snow hummocks that could be covering wheelbarrows or such. The girl had snuffed out the candle before we emerged but the snow itself gave a kind of luminosity and as we skirted what looked like an office block I saw a car waiting in the street beyond. As we approached the driver lifted a hand to the girl, who lifted a hand in return.

"Now I leave you," she said to me. "I wish you good fortune, Comrade."

I thanked her, took her hand for a moment, then she turned away, back to the tunnel entry. The car driver gestured us to get in the back, which we did. The car was a Lada, not very big, which couldn't be said of the chauffeur. She was immense, with beefy shoulders and a large square face and breasts that reached over the steering-wheel and rose and fell over her hands as she turned it. She didn't say a word; just drove and concentrated, but she didn't drive far. In fact only round one corner, into another street where warehouses loomed through the snow, grim and dark and at this hour deserted. The street itself, however, was not deserted. Ahead of us, just around the corner, a figure lurched about, a drunk by the look of him. Our driver slowed and took avoiding action but the snow was hard-packed beneath the powdery surface, no doubt as a result of heavy lorries during the working day, and she skidded, and as she skidded the man lurched again and fell slap in front of us and the Ladybird was unable to avoid him. There was a bump and a scream and then silence.

The driver looked round and backed, the square face impassive. This was no time for the niceties; world peace took precedence over an injured, possibly a dead, drunk. But that was when our luck ran right out: around the corner as we backed away from the body came a police car with headlights beaming. At first its driver didn't see the body, and swung over to pass us; then it checked, turned in for the kerb just past the body, and its roof light came on. As it stopped, an armed policeman got out. Then another. They came towards us, menacingly, one to each front window. I couldn't follow all that was said but got the impression the Ladybird driver wasn't arguing the toss, just stating the fact that what had happened had been unavoidable. Felicity and I stayed silent, hoping, but we both knew it was all up. Soon the police would demand our identification.

They did, and I had hard feelings about all drunks.

We'd had no time to co-ordinate a story. Some while earlier I had agreed false names with Felicity in case of need but I found I had little hope that these would hold up when we were taken, all three of us, to some sort of police district headquarters, not at this stage the Lubyanka itself on Dzerzhinsky Square. We were questioned separately. This was more than a road traffic accident. My interrogator was a squat man, dead Senyavin-shaped but with a mongo-loid face and big hands that kept on clenching and

151

unclenching as though he had ideas of strangulation being the best treatment for Brits. He spoke fair English.

"You say you are English tourist."

"Yes."

"The woman also, the young one."

"Yes."

"With Russian guns," he said smugly.

"Ah yes." It couldn't be denied that this was a poser. There had been no chance of disposing of the machine-pistols. I had to improvise and I did so, keeping a straight face: we had discovered them, I said, abandoned in a back alley and had intended keeping them as souvenirs. I had no idea what Felicity might be saying but had absolutely no faith in my own improvisation, and neither had the interrogator.

"Yes. So many weapons in back alleys in Moscow," he said, full of sarcasm. "Now they are being checked for fingerprints." After that he left the subject alone – I supposed those guns spoke for themselves. He asked, "The other woman, the old one?"

I shrugged. "Just a driver. That's all I know."

"You have no identification, no authority to travel."

"I lost it," I said briefly.

"And the young British woman?"

"And the young lady," I said. I added, "Hers was with mine."

"Yes. Now the vehicle, the Lada. This was not arranged by Intourist."

"No," I said. I yawned involuntarily: I was dead tired; and the bandaged wound in my arm was playing me up too. "A hitch – a lift. A passing motorist . . . we'd got lost. We stopped her and asked for directions."

The squat Mongol glared at me and asked where we had been going and I said the airport.

"To go back to England?"

"Yes."

"Without passports."

152

I said I would have contacted the British Embassy, and asked the man to do just that for me right now. He waved the request aside: there would be no British Embassy, he said. And the airport was nowhere near where we had been picked up. I repeated, with a sigh, that we had got lost.

"Very lost," he said with a smirk. He went away then; I think he was just a menial in police circles, but a menial who had landed something big and meant to pass it on before he put big copper's feet all over a set of tracks and found himself up the creek with his superiors. I was left alone for a long while, locked into the cell where I'd been put, sitting on a wooden plank set into the wall about two feet from the floor. Several times I heard a woman cry out. Felicity or the Ladybird? Or maybe some other woman who'd been picked up. Despondency had settled like a cloud. When they came for me again I was once more joined up with Felicity and the Ladybird. They showed no marks of violence so had probably been treated correctly just as I had been. So far. We were put into a police van under the guns of two guards and the rear door was locked on us and we lurched away slowly over the snow. The van was desperately cold and the guards were warmly wrapped: Felicity and I were not. Our anoraks had been removed and had not been returned. The massive Ladybird woman was all right; she looked as though she was wearing a sheep. None of us spoke during that journey. We just stared at the blank sides and lurched about uncomfortably with the van's movement. At journey's end we were driven into what I saw, when we were ordered out, was a courtyard behind a tall, grim building with tiny windows set in rows, the back of the KGB headquarters, the place of interrogation in depth, the place of silent, thickly-carpeted corridors and individual cells so small that a man could not lie down, the place of terror and hopelessness. By now a dim dawn was in the sky and the snow had stopped falling, though plenty lay on the ground. There was a cold wind that ate through to the bone and swirled the lying snow up in small blizzards, piling it against the bloodstained Lubyanka walls.

Under the guns we were herded towards a doorway. Felicity slipped and fell; she was dragged roughly to her feet by one of the armed policemen, and pushed on again.

We went through the doorway, out of that bitter wind. We entered a square lobby with a man peering through a grille, and an open door on the far side that gave access to a long passage with many other doors leading off it. As we were taken past the grille I saw the man's face disappear and be replaced by that of another man. That man I recognised instantly: the doctor from way back who had stayed behind when we were put in the car with Senyavin and Grulke.

13

The doctor's face had vanished quickly, but our eyes had met and he knew I had recognised him for what that was worth. Once again we were taken to individual cells. But I had a feeling we were not going to remain long in the Lubyanka. The doctor was there for a purpose and that purpose wasn't interrogation. I believed the doctor needed me again and that, to my mind, could mean one thing only: Greenfly was about to go. The official leadership had lost out. The missiles were set to fly. Or anyway, that first of many was.

And somehow the Greenfly boys meant to make use of me.

I thought of that British nuclear submarine on its patrol. I thought of the consternation in the control-room when the interception signal went out, the feeling of helplessness as things started happening around the captain, who would be powerless to interfere with something being directed from outside. Was that how it would come? Or would the whole thing appear normal aboard the submarine, the orders coming through from the Prime Minister – appearing to do so, that was – all the checks answered correctly, the only surprise being that world events had marched so fast since they had left the Faslane base at the start of a routine patrol?

I wasn't left for long this time before I was sent for.

I was taken along a corridor and up in the customary lift into which I was locked with my armed guard in a separate but adjacent compartment. Then along another carpeted corridor and into a small room almost filled by a large desk set in front of a window looking out over snowbound Moscow, a depressing enough scene at the best of times.

My interrogator was an ascetic-looking man in his middle forties, thin, precise, dapper. He had a charming smile and an excellent command of English. And he addressed me as Commander Shaw: of course, he would know all about me from that doctor behind the grille. Having greeted me, he gestured to the armed guard to withdraw and that surprised me even though the door would be guarded from the outside and if I was foolish enough to start anything the guard would be right back in. I was surprised simply because in my experience there is always a strong-arm man present at interrogations.

As matters turned out, I wasn't there to be interrogated. I was there to be informed.

"I understand you are in possession of certain facts, Commander Shaw."

I said nothing; just met his eye and held it. He smiled his friendly smile. "Come now. There are things you'll want to know. Don't be shy of asking."

"All right," I said. "How do you know I'm in possession of any facts at all?"

"Certain persons," he said, and smiled again. "There has been questioning, persuasions, and answers. I'm sure you understand."

I sat silent, thinking. This ascetic Russian could be playing me like a fish: getting me to incrimate Olga Menshikova or Sharef, or dead Comrade Katrina. I wasn't going to assist him in his work of person-destruction.

He went on casually, "You must understand this, we know a great deal about you and your mission, Commander Shaw. There were dead men along the railway track, by the bridge workings. There was a burned-out car on a lonely road. There are the Ladybirds." He smiled once

156

again. "You may unseal your lips, my friend. You can do no-one any harm now."

That was when I asked the question direct. "Are you part of Greenfly?"

"Yes," he answered.

"Right here, inside – ?"

"We have many friends in high places and low ones. The real patriots – "

"And the Soviet leadership, your President?"

"They are hamstrung. We hold the cards. The Soviet Union will be on the march shortly. The march for world power, irresistible. When the first missile lands, the leadership will be forced to respond. Do I need to explain further, Commander Shaw?"

I sat staring at him, staring beyond him to the snow-covered roofs and towers, but I saw none of that. What I saw was the horror of nuclear war, the mushroom clouds, the cindered bodies, the total destruction of crops, of medical aid, of communications, of water supplies, of electricity, of an entire life-system. All for the glorification of Greenfly. I wondered what sort of leadership they would set up, what sort of *Politburo* would emerge to take over from the old guard, as it would have become, in the Kremlin. Not that it would matter to the rest of the shattered world . . . but the Russians themselves would face a pretty bleak future with mad scientists in total charge of all the Soviets. And what this man had said had to be right: when that first British missile landed on Soviet soil, the Kremlin would be able to do nothing but respond with all their nuclear strength, right along the West's borders with communism, and behind them the armoured columns would roll through West Germany, and France, and Holland, the whole continent over-run, and then the air armadas, the hordes of paratroops dropping onto British soil when the fall-out had cleared away. The United States and Canada, those vast land masses, would hold out for longer but they wouldn't in the end withstand the Soviet

157

terror. The Russian submarine fleet would see to that, blasting away its missiles from positions off both the Atlantic and the Pacific seaboards. I knew that in recent years that fleet had been vastly extended both in numbers and in range. It could make rings round the combined British-US submarine services.

That assured, happy smile again. "I see you do understand," the man said. "This will be, as you would say in your country, game, set and match."

I answered with another stupid saying. "There's many a slip. So far as I can see, you're relying on magic. I call that a pretty poor crutch."

"Not magic," he said, shaking his head. "But you shall see for yourself very soon now." He got to his feet; he was a tall man and he blocked my view of the snow, like some evil shadow coming between me and sanity. "When we leave here, we shall be joined by Dr Kholov. We leave at once."

"Before you're rumbled by anyone still loyal to the official leadership, to the Kremlin? You're taking a chance, aren't you? On me, for one?"

He shook his head. "No. If you make a disturbance you will not be believed, you will be considered insane – an Englishman, accusing Soviet citizens . . . but of course there will be a sanction. Just in case you are really insane enough."

I might have known: Felicity. I didn't ask where she was; I saw no point in confirming to this assured man that he had a much valued hostage. For his part, he didn't volunteer any further information.

On the move again: this time in an official KGB car, a staff car, roomy and comfortable. The driver and an armed guard in front; Dr Kholov and me in the back, plus another armed thug and my late interrogator whose name, I gathered, was Siezin. We drove out of Moscow, heading west. There was another car behind us, also a staff car. We drove for a long way, right through the rest of the day. As night came down we were still driving; I had an idea we were going back to the house where I'd been put under the drug, but I was wrong. We continued driving until past midnight, the up-front guard taking turns at the wheel while the driver took his place with the weaponry. On the snowy roads we couldn't make it fast; but Siezin didn't seem worried. I supposed the timing was his own and Kholov's, the only stipulation being that they should go into action before the British submarine returned to base from its patrol, and of course they would be in possession of enough supposedly top secret information to know the timings of the routine patrols. So many moles, so many spies. It had reached the stage today when you couldn't trust anybody. Yesterday's decency and loyalties had all gone now: there was no pride left, no pride in country or job. It was a grab for saleable information, a grab in the interest of some political ism, anything to hit against the state where it wasn't wholly financial. I thought of Radley-Bewick, tainted with that brush, falsely, so that he could become a plant, or a sponge sucking in information from the unsuspecting. That was dirty too – I couldn't deny it. But the Russians were much better at it than the British.

We slowed somewhere in the outskirts of a town – from the signs I saw that it was a place called Lyubytino – and drove off the road through a gateway, stopping behind a sizeable house standing in its own grounds. Ourselves apart, there were no signs of life.

I was ordered out. I climbed out stiffly. The second car pulled in behind us but its passengers stayed put. Siezin brought out a key, went to a door and unlocked it. I was told to follow him in and, with a gun in my back, was pushed into a small room like a cell, with a bed and a barred window. No light: when the door was slammed on me and I could no longer see the light in the passage, I was in total darkness. I hadn't been able to see who was in the second car, and I wondered if Felicity had been one of the passengers. After a short time food and water was brought. I ate and drank in darkness. Then natural urges asserted themselves and I banged on the door. There was no answer. Relief came when my foot clanged against something under the bed. A po. I made use of it and shoved it back under cover. Life was far from comfortable. Like Queen Victoria I lay back on the bed and thought of England.

Eventually I slept, but it was a disturbing sleep, filled with nightmares which woke me sweating after a while and then I couldn't get back to sleep again. My mind was going round in circles: something was nagging at me, something I couldn't pin down – I think I was still in a nightmare of sorts, a half-awake nightmare. I thought about Olga Menshikova and the old retainer. Dead now most probably – the Ladybirds, the true patriots, in disarray. How deep, how far did the Greenfly faction go? It was inconceivable that the men in the Kremlin didn't know what was going on so close beneath their noses – unless Greenfly had got a total grip on affairs, the official leadership being retained for the time being merely as a front. That, in fact, was what it had to be. The West had naturally to be lulled; to keep the softer-line brass intact could be one way of making sure of that. When it was all over, the purges would begin.

And me, and Felicity? We were helpless, no use to anyone. The whole thing had gone sour from the start, from the very moment that original Ladybird had made the stupid, doomed attempt to cross the frontier by Braunlage. And from then on I hadn't been too clever myself. Too trusting? I didn't think so; you had to trust someone and those I'd trusted had kept faith to the point where agony had taken over, and my presence inside Russia had been their destruction.

When the door was unlocked daylight came in. I was brought breakfast and as soon as I had eaten I was taken out again to the car. There was sun now, not very warming but it was a change from the snow. The sky looked clear now. This time I saw Felicity; she was getting into the second car. There was no chance for us to speak and no chance even to catch her eye because she didn't look round. Anyway, I was relieved to see that she was unharmed and to know that we were more or less together.

With the same companions as the day before, we drove out of the gateway, through the town. Siezin had locked the house up on leaving, and once again it stood empty and anonymous. Coming out of Lyubytino we took the road signposted for a place called Nebolchi. For much of the way we ran close to a railway line. Behind the car's glass the sun brought some warmth and the freeze in my bones began to thaw. There was plenty of lying snow and care was still necessary, hence we didn't speed. That snow was piled thickly to the sides of the road: the snow-ploughs had been out before the last fall.

From Nebolchi, which was north of Lyubytino as I saw from the sun's position, we turned west again. West – nearer and nearer, but still so far . . . After Nebolchi the road signs were for Leningrad on the Gulf of Finland.

I asked the question: "Are we heading for Leningrad?"

"Yes," Siezin said.

I was struck by an idea, a theory. I asked, "Are we by any chance going to sea?"

Siezin laughed. "You shall see," he said. He said nothing further, but he murmured something to Dr Kholov, and again there was a laugh. We drove on beneath the climbing sun. The countryside was barren, desolate; under its blanket of snow it was featureless and depressing. Around lunchtime Siezin opened up a hamper that had been brought from the house in Lyubytino, and he and Kholov ate bread and sausage and drank some wine from a bottle. I saw that the driver and the guard were also eating, the latter feeding the former as he drove. Just a happy picnic scene, but I wasn't invited.

It was again dusk as we entered Leningrad. The loom of

161

the city could be seen from far off, an immense spread of light. As we came through the outskirts my mind took a turn towards history: this had once been St Petersburg, capital of the Czarist Russian Empire, setting of the Winter Palace, magnificent even in a city of great palaces filled with treasures. All that glitter had been ended by the revolution; and in more recent times Hitler's armies had come here and the Russians had put up their gallant defence against the Nazi legions so reminiscent of the hordes of Attila the Hun.

As we crossed the Neva River I recalled that it froze from around November to the end of April, but of course there would be icebreakers to assist navigation. As the cars took our party through the streets of industrial Leningrad I could make out away to the right the big cranes and gantries along the loading berths in the port, many of them outlined, as the day darkened, by arc lamps, high-slung yardarm groups over the ships as they took their cargoes or discharged them. A busy scene, even at nightfall. No respite for the docker comrades.

We were not making for the port. We were heading away from it. I felt the tension in the staff car now: Dr Kholov was tapping a hand on the arm rest at his left side and his face had tightened up. Siezin was lying back in his seat, hunched but watchful, eyes everywhere. There was very little traffic for a big seaport and quite soon I saw that we were beginning to come clear of the city, into the outskirts to the south of the Neva, and within the next half-hour we had left Leningrad behind.

It was cold again now, very cold with the onset of the night. I felt the bitter chill as I got out of the car. I stepped out onto ice and would have slid on my backside if the gunman behind me hadn't made a grab in time. Ahead of me there was a bright light which vanished when a door was shut. I had no idea now where we were except that it had to be somewhere on the southern shore of the Gulf of

162

Finland since, in a shaft of moonlight, I could see the glint of water stretching a long way. I could also see Felicity being marched ahead of two men from the second car, towards where the lights had showed.

"Into the building, please," Siezin said from behind me. I moved on, cautiously. The building was long and low, rather like a customs shed. As I got nearer I could see that it was alongside a wharf and I saw also that there was broken ice around a small coaster made fast to bollards on the shore. I knew that the southern fringes of the Gulf of Finland were less susceptible to the freeze than those to the north. It began indeed to look like a sea journey after all. I felt something like a rush of blood to the head: at sea, we would at least be outside the land barriers of the Soviet Union and never mind that we would be aboard, presumably, a Soviet vessel.

It would be a kind of freedom.

Currently there wasn't much freedom aspect. I was marched into the shed, into the source of the bright light. There were packing cases around and about a dozen men waiting, wrapped to the eyeballs in warm clothing. Siezin went across and spoke to them. Some were wearing what looked like uniform trousers under the wrappings, others were not. Some wore high boots. I got the impression this was a mix of KGB, Soviet Navy and merchant seamen. Dr Kholov started checking the crates, numbering them off or something, accompanied by two of the waiting men. When he had finished he gave a nod and the men, those not in any particular uniform, began manhandling them out of the shed and into the open by the wharf. Soon after this I heard the sound of machinery, either a dockside crane or the ship's winches putting them aboard, and when the sounds ceased one of the men came back inside and reported to Siezin.

Siezin gestured towards me. "We go aboard now," he said.

I was marched with the others up a narrow gangway

163

whence I dropped down to the ship's foredeck. The crates, lashed down and covered with canvas tarpaulins, had been set on top of the hatches to form a deck cargo. I was taken into the after superstructure and pushed into a small cabin with no port, and locked in. I had seen Felicity go aboard ahead of me but had then lost sight of her. Soon after I had been locked up I heard the sounds of the ship getting under way, the ropes and wires being cast off and brought inboard, the ring of the engineroom telegraph from time to time as we manoeuvred off the berth, then ahead and on course through the sandbanks and the broken ice and the many, many islands that dotted the Gulf of Finland, heading presumably for the wider waters of the Baltic beyond Tallinn.

Dr Kholov evidently meant to make his interception from seaward – I'd got as far as the obvious. But it wasn't until the engines slowed and then stopped some hours later and I was taken on deck beneath a cold but calm dawn that I saw what Kholov's transmission base was to be. We had stopped alongside a black shape low in the water, the conning tower rearing like an immense fin, sinister beneath that dawn that might well be the last before the northern hemisphere disintegrated, stopped alongside a nuclear-powered hunter-killer, one of the USSR's attack submarines.

14

I knew that the Russian missile-launching submarines were based not in the Gulf of Finland but with the Northern Fleet at Murmansk on the Kola inlet; if they were anything like the British ones they would be immense: three-deck-level jobs, their displacement tonnage not far off that of the old World War Two cruisers. The attack submarines were a lot smaller, which stood to reason: I couldn't be sure, but I doubted if the missile monsters would find an easy passage submerged through the narrows into the Kattegat and the open sea and in this connection I was making two logical assumptions: that Kholov wouldn't be transmitting long distance from inside the Baltic, and that we were meant to proceed outwards submerged, both of which assumptions were later confirmed by Comrade Siezin.

We all clambered aboard the casing, aboard the fore deck, slithering on the ice, holding tight to the lifelines that guided us towards a hatch in the base of the conning tower.

We entered a warm world, a world that hummed electrically about our ears. Shining steel ladders, plastic-covered steel decks, steel bulkheads, alleyways shimmering into the distance beneath the glaring electric bulbs, alleyways that were broken up by watertight doors currently standing open. The sub's captain came down from the conning tower in person to welcome Siezin aboard. This was all very official, unless the captain had also been suborned by Greenfly and was willing to take the risk on something that he believed would be no risk at all once Greenfly won out. Another rat, leaving the sinking ship of state? Greenfly was probably the better prospect now.

The moment all the crates had been transferred and brought down through a big loading hatch in the after casing, the submarine got under way and I was taken with Dr Kholov to what was plainly the control-room. There was a mass of computerised equipment, bank upon bank of keyboards, screens, dials, gauges . . . green flickering light and a continual *ping-ping* as a rating seated before one of the screens moved a milled-edged wheel.

Siezin was currently absent. But Felicity was brought in and told to sit on a let-down stool. Then I was told to sit on a similar stool on the opposite side of the control-room from Felicity. At a word from an officer, two armed seamen moved in, one behind each of us.

There was silence except for some distant banging: the crates, I supposed. The control-room itself, apart from the pinging sound, was extraordinarily quiet, almost a cathedral hush, and somehow antiseptic. You couldn't imagine a good old seafaring British cockroach having the temerity to butt in. I thought of what I'd heard about the old conventionally-powered submarines, tin cigars with all hands living cheek by jowl in what you would now call squalor, in dim and fetid air and clothing that wasn't changed for the duration of a whole patrol. And every smell imaginable: oil, battery acid, cooking, grease . . . it had been pretty abominable really but the atmosphere, if thick, had always been cheerful. Or so I'd been told. I wouldn't have called this cheerful: the faces were grim and tense, the eyes watchful. They couldn't, I supposed, be blamed: when you were about to start a train of events that would shatter more than forty years of peace you were bound to tense up a little.

There was a clatter on the ladder. Siezin came down. He gave me a speculative glance. A second man came down behind, and Siezin turned towards him, then spoke to me.

"This is Comrade Smith," he said.

Comrade Smith: the name meant nothing to me. He was a nondescript little bloke who grinned, rather sheepishly I thought, and said, "Cheers." Then I ticked over: the name of the defector of whom Katrina had told me had not in fact been Smith; but any name would do if you wanted to make the change and I guessed that Comrade Smith was the scientist from the Ministry of Defence, the man with personal and detailed knowledge of the missile-firing submarines of the British Navy, the man who was going to do his screen-test stuff. I would have thought his presence rendered my own obsolete, but supposed they had to do something with me now they'd got me back. I couldn't have been allowed to wander off and alert the West, after all.

I nodded at Comrade Smith's greeting but didn't say anything in response. A few moments later orders came down from the conning tower and the submarine increased speed, the hum of the motors rising to a high whine for a while before settling down. Soon after that a number of ratings were to be seen moving along the alleyway from for'ard, manhandling Kholov's crates into the control-room, a proceeding which the doctor watched over with an eagle eye, clicking his tongue at intervals and urging, as I took it to be, care. Once the heavy crates were positioned he began unpacking and arranging his set-up. Out came a screen and a bird's-nest of electric leads, a square metal box with a number of dials and knobs, and an assortment of other gear. The medical side was there as well: hypodermics, phials, electrodes, sachets and so on. But this time no nurse. Comrade Smith was looking at the hypodermics and I fancied there was a worried aspect, and I laughed.

Comrade Smith looked at me. "What's funny?" he asked.

I shrugged. "Oh, nothing. But it won't hurt. And I'll tell you something else for free: it won't work either."

"Perhaps it didn't, with you."

I lifted an eyebrow. "You know about that, do you?"

"Yes. But I know more than you do. Up to a point, it did work. With you."

Maybe he was right; there had been that weird semi-dream and then Senyavin's, or had it been the doctor's, subsequent satisfaction with my performance under deep drug therapy, if such was the word. I still didn't know how I'd reacted, not for sure. I looked at Comrade Smith again. I asked, "So now it's your turn to go into a trance, is it?"

"It's not a trance exactly."

"Well, never mind the precise term," I said, and looked him up and down. "What about the moral aspect?"

He flushed a little. He was a pale-faced man, spotty, and the flush showed. He said, "How moral is political life in the West, for God's sake?"

"I wouldn't link God with this, Comrade. You've gone over to anti-Christ. I won't insult your intelligence by asking you if you really understand what the result's going to be. Have you any family?" I recollected from the press reports at the time that in fact he had: elderly parents and a sister. Never been married.

He said defensively, "Yes, I have."

"But you didn't consider them."

"Family feelings can't be allowed to stand in the way. It was the same in wartime, wasn't it?"

I said, "Not quite, but I get your point. You're going to be a big boy in the Soviet Union, aren't you? The man who gave communism its biggest boost . . . you'll never starve, will you, Comrade Smith? Hero of the Soviet Union, along with Dr Kholov. Red carpet treatment here on out. Taking the salute from the Kremlin wall, with all the ageing brass. That's if it all goes according to plan. What if it doesn't, Comrade Smith?"

He said, "Oh, it's not going to fail, believe me," and then he turned away, back to Kholov, who was showing signs of impatience at our conversation. Left to my thoughts again, I tried to make an assessment of where we might be heading and when we would get there. The speed . . . thirty knots probably – they wouldn't be lingering at this stage. I believed thirty knots to be the maximum available to the British nuclear-powered submarines either surfaced or submerged, but possibly the Russians had more. Anyway at thirty knots for most of the way, and allowing for a probably slow and careful passage of the narrows, and assuming we were currently somewhere off Tallinn, I reckoned that inside forty-eight hours we could be somewhere off the Western Approaches above the Bay of Biscay. We would have all Biscay and the North Atlantic as a hunting ground, the objective being, obviously, one of the British submarines on its sixty-day patrol, the one that was going to be made to loose off its missiles.

Of course, the patrol areas were top secret: weren't they? I gave a hollow laugh. Comrade Siezin looked round, lifting an eyebrow but not commenting. Comrade Siezin would have all the answers. I wondered once again if anything at all was secret now. In the Kremlin, or in the heart of Greenfly, they probably knew how many times the British captain in the target submarine changed his socks . . .

I wondered which of our submarine fleet it would be. *Renown, Repulse, Revenge, Resolution?* Oldies now, but those were the names that came to mind. I wondered what confusing thoughts I might dream up if I was connected again to the screen.

It was an hour later when the captain came down from the conning tower and the two planesmen took up their stations for controlling the depth and angle of the boat. The ship's company went to diving stations; the periscope was sent up and the captain put his eye to it. Now the course was SSW. We would be moving down past the islands off the coast of Estonia to come between the USSR and Gotland and on to the narrows and the Kattegat. The Swedes or

169

the Danes, probably both, were bound of course to pick us up on their detectors; I asked Comrade Siezin about that and he laughed: *they* wouldn't interfere, he said, but didn't go into any explanation and I was left with the reflection that the USSR was a very big, powerful and angry neighbour. I remarked that the passage of the narrows would be tricky.

"Not so," Siezin said. "Our navigators know the area well. So much practice."

I nodded. "Sure. You've never given a damn for the sanctity of territorial rights, have you?"

"There is no sanctity of these waters, the passage is free – ships of many nations enter the Baltic and the Gulf of Finland through the Kattegat."

But, I thought to myself, war vessels on clandestine missions are a different kettle of fish . . . as if anticipating my next query Comrade Siezin went on, "You may think it would have been easier if we had used a missile-firing submarine from Murmansk."

"The thought did cross my mind. Freer waters and all that. More direct."

"Yes. Navigationally . . . not politically."

I got his point. "You mean the Murmansk naval command is with the official Kremlin, not with Greenfly?"

"For now yes. Afterwards it will be different."

"You hope," I said. Nothing more from Comrade Siezin. The submarine was now down to the depth setting ordered by the captain and was away through the Baltic for the narrows and eventually the Skagerrak and the North Sea and the final act. Food was brought for us soon after this. We sat there in the control-room and ate, Felicity and me, Dr Kholov, Comrades Siezin and Smith, and the guards who had come in the car from Moscow. I had little appetite even though I was in fact in want of food. Siezin went into an expansive mood; it was partly his confidence that put me off thoughts of eating.

170

"It will not be long," he said, as satisfied as a happy cat. "Not as time goes."

"And afterwards you'll have all the time in the world."

He nodded. "Yes."

"Plans already made, of course," I said. "I refer to the situation in Moscow – in the Kremlin. Your lot takes over – right?"

Again Siezin nodded. "When the reports come in from the north. As soon as the missiles strike, the Soviets will be ready under their new leadership."

"And you, Comrade Siezin? You'll be stuck aboard this boat. Out of communication. Suppose someone takes advantage of that?" I didn't for a moment suppose that there was all that much love and loyalty between the individual members of Greenfly. If Comrade Siezin had ideas of himself assuming the Soviet leadership then he might be confounded by one of his own mates, beaten in the race by a comrade on the spot in Moscow. "But I suppose you'll have thought of that, won't you?"

There was an indifferent shrug. "It will not happen. And I shall not be out of communication as you suggest."

"You'll surface afterwards?"

"Perhaps. I do not yet know. The situation must itself dictate, Commander Shaw. But I can of course communicate in any event and I shall be in a position to take radio reports from my bureau in Moscow even when submerged." Siezin went on to explain that the missile submarines, though forbidden ever to transmit whilst on patrol, could receive signals even when submerged at great depths and the same applied, he said, to this submarine. This was achieved by means of a wire streamed on the surface and capable of receiving VHF transmissions. It was by means of this wire, Siezin said, that in a war situation the firing orders would be expected to reach the missile submarines from the capital concerned – Moscow, London, Washington as the case might be. As it happened

171

I was well aware of this but had let Siezin go on in case he revealed something useful.

But he didn't. He yacked politics and world domination while he ate. After a while I asked him what he intended doing with me and Felicity. That was a mistake; I'd meant to ask him where we fitted into his missile-launching scheme now that Comrade Smith was present but he took my question the wrong way. He said, "Afterwards you will be superfluous to our requirements. I think I need not elaborate."

I took a quick look at Felicity, wishing I'd not opened my mouth. She was as white as a sheet. But it should have been obvious, of course.

I could find nothing whatever that either of us could do about anything. We were helpless. Just the two of us against a submarine's dedicated complement plus Siezin's personal bodyguard, moving south towards destiny beneath the Baltic waves. I even felt past prayer; if God intended doing anything he would already have made his mind up. Felicity and I . . . we were already superfluous. Or so I thought. That turned out to be wrong: Siezin and Kholov, when they'd finished eating, went into conference. There was a lot of quiet discussion out of my earshot, many nods and gestures, and then Siezin announced that there was to be a preliminary run through, a kind of dress rehearsal.

I was put under the drug again. So was Comrade Smith; I was roped down on a mattress placed across the deck of the control-room. The screen had been rigged along one of the bulkheads. We were festooned with electrodes. The periscope was down in its housing now: the submarine had gone deep but was maintaining its speed, so far as I knew until the drug had taken effect and though fully conscious had lost awareness of such mundane details. It was back to the mental processes, the projection on the screen. My own thoughts showed as a jumble: ship names, one after the other, the names of the missile fleet. Black hulls making their way down the Firth of Clyde past the Cumbraes, past the Sound of Bute, past Arran . . . I couldn't keep my thoughts free of what was upmost in my mind, although I tried to force them onto something more innocuous. My efforts did have the effect of a blur, but in any case neither Kholov or Siezin appeared much interested in my submarine reflections. I heard, as through a daze, the voice of Dr Kholov urging politics and Downing Street and the Ministry of Defence on me. As a result, some images came through; but they were flickering, insubstantial. Crowds outside Number Ten, yelling for the Prime Minister's blood because war loomed. Peace marchers doing much the same outside the House of Commons. And back into history: a pugnacious man in a funny black hat that was a mix of topper and bowler, holding up two fingers in a rude gesture. That sort of thing. It didn't appear to be of much use and Kholov hissed angrily. I was disconnected from the screen. Comrade Smith came on in my place. I hadn't been put under so deeply as last time, back inside Russia itself, and I was able to watch the reflected thoughts of our British defector.

As with me, it was the Firth of Clyde to begin with: a nuclear-powered submarine, out of Faslane presumably, moving along fast beneath a clear blue sky. The sea was calm and there was snow on the heights of Arran above Lamlash. Ahead, also snow-covered, was the great rock of Ailsa Craig. There was no ship name on the hull but every now and again a word appeared as Comrade Smith thought on: *Iron Duke*. So it was to be HMS *Iron Duke*, one of our latest class. Like *Revenge* and *Resolution* the previous vessel of that name had been a battleship. Long before my time but I knew of them. *Emperor of India*, *Benbow*, *Marlborough*, *Iron Duke*. *Iron Duke* had been the flagship of the Grand Fleet in World War One, had ended her career as an accommodation ship off Lyness in Scapa, filled with concrete as a result of some of Hitler's bombs in World War Two, fixed to the sea bed – the tide used to

173

rise round her. Powerful in her day, but a fleabite as compared with her current namesake.

Comrade Smith threw the current *Iron Duke*'s control-room onto the screen. I saw men moving about, tending things, reading dials. Then the control room vanished and up came another scene: Comrade Smith's thoughts produced the words Missile Control Centre. I saw an officer, a lieutenant-commander, holding a pistol-grip trigger. The missile firer? Then there was another shift: the new one looked like the wardroom, a group of rather formless-faced officers in white, open-neck shirts with shoulder-straps, playing cards. Mostly smoking cigarettes. One of them wore the scarlet cloth of the medical branch between his gold stripes, a surgeon lieutenant. I assumed these to be the officers with whom Comrade Smith had sailed when he'd taken his submerged trip. All this was merely historic: even the name didn't really *have* to be that of the target submarine. More of the content of Comrade Smith's mind was thrown onto the screen: a jumble of things largely, but they gradually sorted out again and the context told me we were still with HMS *Iron Duke*.

Kholov was growing impatient: he had a word with Siezin, who nodded and frowned. Some of Kholov's explanations to me back in his laboratory or whatever came vividly to me through the haze produced by the drug. He'd said I'd been able to mingle with the wavelength, with the thoughts and actions, the current thoughts and actions, of the people of whom I was thinking, that I was a vehicle for what was not quite extra-sensory perception. I was not required exactly to prophesy; I would not be programmed for that. *An eavesdropping of the conscious mind* – that was what Kholov had said. He'd quoted Socrates: in dreams the soul can apprehend what it does not know. But I had been, and was now, *awake*. My mind, according to Kholov, was able to apprehend, like the soul in dreams, what it did not know . . .

"The element is precognosis," I said aloud.

Kholov swung round on me. I said, "You told me that, Dr Kholov."

He nodded. "Yes. And I answered, when you suggested that I meant telepathy, that it was indeed telepathy of a kind. I – "

"Induced telepathic ability."

"That is correct. And the precognosis element is of the present. Not the future. That is the nub."

"And Comrade Smith," I said, "isn't getting there. He's missing the nub – isn't he?"

Smith was still being historic. He himself appeared in his screen-depicted thoughts and that, to me, was the proof that he wasn't with the present. He couldn't be in two places at once . . . I began to laugh. This thing wasn't going to work out. It was obvious the test, the rehearsal, wasn't going well. Kholov rounded on me, his temper showing, and brought the back of a hand across my face, twice. He didn't like being laughed at. He said that, in any case, I would see that there was nothing to laugh about. Not for me. There was time in hand yet, he said.

I thought about that wire streamed on the surface above the submerged submarine. Would Comrade Siezin send his orders by radio, the firing orders as from Whitehall, for reception via the VHF wire streamed from the *Iron Duke*?

Unlikely, very. The form of the firing order really would be secret: no agent would have a hope of ever getting inside knowledge of that. Besides, any interference signal of that sort would be picked up in Whitehall and in the headquarters of C-in-C Fleet at Northwood, and an immediate cancellation would be issued in the midst of the sheer panic that would grip the government, and in the general confusion the captain of the *Iron Duke* would naturally play safe.

Wouldn't he? In point of fact it would be quite a decision to have to make. Which side would he consider authentic? He might well decide that the moment had come to

175

disregard the absolute order that said he must never transmit whilst on patrol: he might ask for clarification. After that it would again depend on his own assessment, his interpretation of the answers that he would get from Whitehall and from Comrade Siezin. But there was still the question of Siezin getting the form right – that was still highly unlikely. Very big, very lethal rats would be smelled aboard the *Iron Duke*. However, that streamed wire remained on my mind. It didn't show on the screen since I was disconnected; Comrade Smith was still in the hot seat. Kholov was now squatting by his side on the deck, talking quietly into his ear, and another injection had been given. And there was a vital difference now. We were still with the *Iron Duke* but we were not in the wardroom and there was no sign of Smith in the picture. It was all much more immediate, somehow. And there were different, sharper faces among the officers – there was a different captain for one.

I felt my flesh creep, almost literally. I had a feeling Kholov and Siezin really were getting somewhere. I had a feeling that via Comrade Smith's drug-induced coma or whatever it was, we were seeing inside the *Iron Duke* on her current patrol. A strong degree of triumph seemed to be sparking between Kholov and Siezin. In the screen-depicted Missile Control Centre I saw the combination-lock safe containing the pistol-grip that would start the last war of all. My understanding was that two officers, the captain and one other, were required to bring together, from different safes with different combinations, authentication cards to check the war signal from C-in-C Fleet – a fact that should finally dispose of any interference possibility. *Should dispose* . . . but Kholov and Siezin were growing more confident by the minute.

Then, via Smith, I saw on the screen the navigation chart of the *Iron Duke*. I saw her current position marked. So did Comrade Siezin. He turned round and said, "She is in the North Sea. Off the Firth of Forth, between there and the Skagerrak."

Which was considerably nearer to our own position than I'd been bargaining for.

15

I said, "There'll come a time when she'll pick us up, Comrade Siezin. Her sonar – "

"Her captain will not be alarmed or surprised. Such will have happened before. From time to time the patrol areas cross as between the Soviet and the British and American missile submarines."

If only we hit her, I thought. Many lives might be lost, mine and Felicity's included, but world tragedy would be avoided. I didn't know how close Comrade Siezin needed to be, but I thought it wouldn't need to be all that close considering that Smith had brought it all up so clearly already, and probably Siezin could give a go at any moment. I asked him: at this stage he wouldn't see any reason to hold back.

He said, "We must wait for an exercise, Commander Shaw."

"An exercise?"

"Each patrolling submarine exercises a missile launch at intervals of a few days at most. An exercise signal comes from Northwood and all short of the actual launch is enacted just as though it was real."

"You know it all, don't you," I said bitterly.

"I think so, yes," Siezin answered with full confidence. "And, you see, when the exercise is at its height – when the signal, the real and true signal for exercise has been made and received, and the authentication has been given by the responsible officers, and the pistol-grip has been produced from the final safe – "

"All of which you'll learn from Smith?"

Siezin nodded. "Yes. Everything will have been prepared for us. With the pistol ready to be squeezed . . . that is when we make our interference. That is when, from this submarine, we send off the missiles."

I asked, "How do you put them on course? How do you direct them where *you* want, rather than wherever they might be targeted for?"

Siezin smiled. "Always they are targeted on Russia! That is what they are for, is it not?"

"But the remote areas, the northern shores where there aren't many people? They won't be targeted up that way, will they?"

Siezin smiled again and met the eye of Dr Kholov. "They can be re-directed in flight," he said. There was some curious undertone in his voice; and I didn't believe him. I believed he didn't care whereabouts in Russia the missiles landed, I believed that so long as he had his way and put Greenfly on top, he didn't care how many of his countrymen died. And I believed that, rather naturally, he didn't want the men aboard the submarine to know this. They wouldn't want their families, scattered over many parts of Russia presumably, to suffer. They might mutiny. It was just possible in any case that none of them except maybe the captain knew what Siezin was doing. They could have been hoodwinked – that wouldn't have been difficult. Russians do what they're told in the main. All the conversation between Smith and me, and between the Russians and me, had been in English and the ratings in the proximity hadn't shown the least sign of understanding. I began to feel the onset of something not far removed from panic: this whole set-up, basically so weird, so way out, so impossible, was taking on the aspect of reality, of something that could happen – was going to happen. The British, next time the exercise signal went out from C-in-C Fleet for a dummy run, would play straight into Siezin's hands, preparing the way for him.

It was all so simple, if you accepted those extra-sensory powers given to Comrade Smith. I both did and didn't: it went way beyond my experience and my belief but I had myself been put under that drug, back in Russia – much more deeply under than this time aboard the submarine – and I remembered the sensation, the rocking of my mind, of my whole mental balance, as though, before I'd gone under and out, I was being drawn away from the reality of time and place, that my mind had left my body and had settled, hovering, somewhere . . . where Senyavin, now dead, had wanted it to be, where Dr Kholov, here present and very much alive, had wanted it to be.

I looked around at the maze of instruments, the computers, the electric circuits, the dials, the flickering green lights, the taped leads connecting Comrade Smith's mind and brain to the screen. A bull in a china shop was what was wanted. I wouldn't have a chance, of course, of playing that role. Nor would Felicity. She was now handcuffed to a ringbolt set into a bulkhead, well away from all the vital parts; and I was tied down to my mattress still. I didn't know even now what part I was expected to play but assumed there must be something lined up. I looked at the screen, at the enlarged end-product of Comrade Smith's deeply drugged mind.

It still showed normality as yet, the routine of a long patrol.

It hopped about a little: ratings at the various controls, the planesmen watching their dial readings, hands lightly on the aircraft-type wheels that kept the boat trimmed to the orders of the officer of the watch behind them. Then the wardroom, with the off-watch officers reading, yawning. The bunks set throughout the boat, some with men asleep. The galley, the wireless room, the surgery, the main machinery space, the messdeck set with tables. Then, again, the Missile Control Centre, all very quiet and peaceful. Yet, to me, brooding, the calm before the storm. It could be a long calm. It would depend on when the last exercise firing had been signalled. Siezin had spoken of an exercise every few days. Not that it mattered. Armageddon would come sooner or later. I was convinced of that now. There would be no avoidance; when we surfaced again it would be to a shattered world. We might even remain submerged until the fall-out had cleared away. We would have the capacity to do just that. But it would be up to Comrade Siezin, of course; he might want to be in Moscow, asserting the fact of Greenfly's takeover from the old guard.

A man entered the control-room and I looked up at him and saw import as he approached the captain. A lot of time had passed now and I had been told we had entered the Skagerrak some while earlier and were moving out fast into the North Sea, approaching the position as estimated of the *Iron Duke* on her patrol. There was a brief conversation between the captain and the newcomer and a sheet of paper was handed over. The captain caught Comrade Siezin's eye and passed the paper to him. I saw the sudden consternation in Siezin's face. He and Kholov went into a huddle with the captain. I couldn't catch anything that was being said but it seemed there could be a spanner in the works. After a few moments Siezin came away from the group and approached me. It seemed my services were required. I was untied from the mattress and, with a gun in my back, I was led out of the control-room and taken to the wireless office.

Questions. I refused to answer them and the rough stuff started. After five minutes I was pretty groggy: I had been hit repeatedly, with fists and gun-barrels, all over my body. Comrade Siezin was a right bastard and he was angry. And worried: there had been a signal, that piece of paper. It had come in from one of Siezin's lot – a naval Greenfly supporter infiltrated into the Russian naval base at Murmansk. A transmission from London had been picked up by the Russian monitors. There had been a number of corrupt groups – it was a cyphered message, but the

Russians had the means of breaking cyphers and they'd broken this one. The corrupt groups were so many that in fact they hadn't got much out of it, but what they had got Siezin's plant had passed on. And what brought me into it was 6D2. It had been a 6D2 cypher.

And, of course, Comrade Siezin had spent his WUS-WIPP years fighting us in 6D2. He wanted to know what the signal meant.

"I can't help," I said.

"I believe you can. You can fill in the missing parts."

"I'm not psychic," I pointed out. "Why not try Comrade Smith?"

That was when Siezin began to lose his temper, and lashed out at me. My head rocked backwards but I stayed on my feet. "I am asking you. You will do as I say. First I wish to know to whom the signal is addressed."

I glanced down again at the transcript, what there was of it: even the addressee was corrupt, hence his first query. The body of the message contained a reference to myself and Miss Mandrake, only Siezin wasn't to know that since Max, who would presumably have been the originator, had used code names. The place-name Braunlage had come across in the decyphering and there was a reference to Hans Schulz, to Greenfly, and to Moscow; also to the Supreme Soviet.

That was about all. It foxed me as well as Comrade Siezin, and I said so. It crossed my mind that the message could have been addressed to Radley-Bewick, who had died only very recently. The news of his death wouldn't necessarily have reached London yet. Or if it had, then the message might have been addressed to another of our men inside Russia and could have referred to the death. All that, however, was supposition. But I still wasn't going to assist Siezin, even with guesswork. Frankly, I saw no particular reason for all the anxiety in Siezin's vicious face. He held all the cards. He was set to take over. I didn't

182

imagine Max could do anything about that. No more than I could . . .

Siezin said, "You know the mind of 6D2. You know the way your people work. You will interpret the signal."

Again I said I couldn't. Something hard took me in the kidney region, and I doubled. I was brought upright again by a hard blow to the jaw. Then my legs were kicked away from beneath me and I went flat on the deck. Next my head was kicked and I saw bright lights, flashes, stars. When I tried to drag myself up by a hand on a metal shelf, the hand was almost squashed to bloody pulp by the butt of a sub-machine gun wielded by one of Siezin's thugs. The gunshot wound in my arm opened up again beneath the bandage. In the end I was saved by the bell: more vital matters supervened when a telephone burred and Siezin himself answered it.

The *Iron Duke* was going into exercise firing.

I was taken back, almost carried back, to the control-room where I was thrown to the deck in a heap at Felicity's feet.

Exercise firing was a lengthy process and a fraught one; no doubt exercises could always go wrong. Even from the screen I could feel the tension inside the *Iron Duke*. At first sight Comrade Smith had looked already dead. His face was white and strained, with black circles beneath the eyes, and his only movement was a facial twitch that began soon after I had been brought back. Then he started very heavy breathing, came out with abundant sweat that ran down his face and neck. He was like a leaf, shivering violently all over. He was covered with more electrodes now, some leading to the screen, others leading to Dr Kholov's extra-sensory perception control box, for want of a better name. Another box, a largish cabinet in fact, stood ready behind one of the planesmen with Comrade Siezin in charge of it. On top of the box was a metal plate and in Siezin's right hand there was a thin bar, also of metal, like a biro, connected at one end to a socket in the side of the box. From the box another electric lead ran to some of the submarine's gadgetry. I made a series of guesses: when Siezin brought the biro-like bar down, touched it against the metal plate, the submarine would, using its own power and communications system perhaps, transmit to the *Iron Duke*. The transmission would interrupt the exercise at the critical moment, activating the firing lever of the pistol which by then would be held by the *Iron Duke*'s captain. From then on the exercise would be for real.

Siezin glanced down at me and our eyes met. From the corner of one of mine I was aware of the man with the sub-machine gun, the latter aimed at me and held close. Siezin laughed. He said, "Perhaps you follow what is to happen." He seemed to have forgotten about the signal now.

I said, "Perhaps I do." As that message came to mind I had a sudden flash of hope that something had leaked out of Russia, something that had caused Max to make the signal. If that was the case then he might even now be doing his best to persuade the fleet headquarters in Northwood to negate the exercise and bring the *Iron Duke* to the surface. But it was a very slim hope: the leak would have had to be very comprehensive to make Max connect a Russian submarine into the picture. I had another hope, an even slimmer one, that the *Iron Duke*'s missiles would not be armed with their warheads. Of course they would be; that was the whole point of the patrols – instant readiness for war. There were procedures to inhibit any accidental firings. And just then, as though in tune with my thoughts, Siezin went into some explanations as to what was going to take place.

He said, "When I transmit, which will be at a very exact moment, I shall by-pass the British procedures, the fail-safe interlockings that would normally prevent the discharge of the missiles. Do you understand?"

"I follow the theory," I said. "To put it into practice may be a different thing. Don't you agree?"

"There will be no hitch." Siezin was very confident.

I said from my position on the deck, "This'll be for the first time – obviously. You haven't done it for real before. With any luck, you'll blow yourself up instead."

Siezin didn't bother to answer that. He was concentrating on the screen now, on Comrade Smith's transmitted revelations as the defector's mind roved around aboard the *Iron Duke*. Smith was in fact doing well. The whole thing, the whole sequence of the exercise, was being shown to us in its entirety, and Smith's voice, sounding hollow and detached, was repeating the orders as they came.

I heard him say, "Authentication procedure." I assumed that the cyphered exercise signal from C-in-C Fleet had come in whilst I was with Siezin in the wireless room and was now being checked out. Then the screen showed one of *Iron Duke*'s officers, a lieutenant-commander, manipulating the combination lock of a safe. The door swung open to reveal another safe, which was then opened by another officer. A card was withdrawn from each safe, and each was checked against the cypher from fleet HQ.

Smith's voice said, "Authenticated, both halves. Time, 0233."

Then the cards were replaced and the safes locked with twirls of the combination handles. I saw the officers walk away and then the scene shifted to the control-room. There was an officer wearing the three gold stripes of a commander: the *Iron Duke*'s captain. There was a quiet alertness, total calm, eyes watching dials and gauges, watching the trim of the boat. A rating was picking his nose, a reflex action as his mind concentrated. The captain stood motionless, watching everything, no idea in his mind as to what was going to happen as the exercise drew to its climax, what was going to take place in the world above the waves. As for me, I was fascinated to the point of being oblivious of my own surroundings. As I watched the screen the background shifted again, this time to the fore casing, and I saw the sixteen round hatch-covers over the

185

missiles. They were still closed. I wondered if, under exercise conditions, they remained closed or whether to open them was part of the exercise routine, the whole thing running right through for test, right to the point just short of the actual firing. If they didn't open . . . well, the world would be safe for a while longer and the 140 men of the *Iron Duke*'s company would never know what had happened when the whole lot blew inside the pressure hull. Fancifully I wondered what would happen to the detached mind of Comrade Smith. We might be left with a mindless body that still lived. Unless minds didn't fragment like material . . .

Back once again to the control-room.

The two officers depicted earlier were entering the compartment and reporting to the captain that the Northwood signal had been authenticated.

There was a nod from the captain. Smith said in that disembodied voice, "Missiles to full readiness." One of the officers moved away and Smith tracked him to the Missile Control Centre. Here a third safe was opened. Out came the 64,000-dollar object: a revolver-like grip connected to a cable leading through to the back of the safe. Its trigger was painted red.

The firing mechanism: suddenly, despite the warm fug inside the submarine, I felt deadly cold. Instinctively I lifted myself on an elbow. The man with the sub-machine gun pushed me down, brutally. The muzzle of the gun stayed close to my mouth.

The control-room again: Smith's mind was busy. I looked up at Comrade Siezin. His eyes were blazing, his face working with his excitement, his inner thrill that Greenfly was all set to go, that the Soviet would be finally forced into war, the prelude to total world control. I wondered if the Greenfly boys, spread out around the Russian land mass, many of them in positions of authority no doubt, were intending to let go the Russian missiles in retaliation, long before London and Washington had ticked over. It would be a case of pants well and truly round the ankles of the collective West. There was undoubtedly a rationale behind the mad-sounding schemes of Greenfly.

On the screen I saw the captain again. Smith's voice came: "Stand by to hover . . . stop engines." There was a pause then he uttered again. "Hull-valve open." There was something about auto, and reference to a computer, but I didn't catch it all before Smith switched us back to the Missile Control Centre, where a rating was seen making what looked like a series of checks, pressing a number of buttons. As he did so green lights came up and he reported, to someone not in the picture, "Gyros, battery, power and alignment correct. Spinning." More checks, and then we were given another sight of the fore casing. Out there in the water, I thought to myself, Smith's mind might drown, but no such luck. And I saw the sixteen hatches: the covers were open now.

All ready. And back to the control-room. An officer wore a headset and was listening intently, his face taut, almost as if he'd sensed the reality behind the exercise. After a moment this officer made a report.

The captain responded, as relayed by Comrade Smith: "Permission to fire." He reached into the neck of his white uniform shirt and pulled out a key on a length of codline. The key was painted red, like the trigger of the firing pistol. With this he moved across the control-room towards a board set overhead. He locked the key into a slot in this board.

This, I believed, was it. Or almost it: it was, I believed, the moment when the exercise would end, the moment when reality would supervene. Kholov was watching closely. Smith's mind, aboard the *Iron Duke*, next depicted a panel with a red light and some words stencilled onto it. As I watched, the light and the words turned green. They were the final permission to fire. I saw Siezin's hand hovering with the metal pointer, and starting to bring it down on the circular plate above his control box.

187

Siezin had to choose his moment exactly, very precisely right – so he had said. But I believed that he had enough leeway, just so long as he made his firing contact, sent it out through the depths of the ocean to penetrate the hull of the *Iron Duke* and complete the circuit by interference, before the captain brought the exercise to a stop. I, too, chose my moment – better late than never for a desperate last throw that had all the odds against it.

I made a fast squirm sideways. The man guarding me was intent, like all the others, on the screen as the last few seconds fled away, and he wasn't quite fast enough to stop me as I flung myself on Comrade Smith. Even so there was a degree of speed about him and he did my work for me. I felt the heat of lead passing close, nipping my left ear-lobe to bring a downpour of blood. It was Comrade Smith who took that burst of sub-machine gun fire, most of it in his head. As the compartment filled with the acrid stench of the gunsmoke the screen went blank and in the same instant Siezin touched his metal biro down onto the circular plate.

We were out of all contact now; dead Smith's mind was gone, had maybe rejoined his body at the last all ready to part company again in the normal fashion of death, en route for the next world. Or perhaps it was still out there in the ocean depths, trying crazily, vainly, to transmit more messages that now would never be received. Aboard the Russian submarine there was anger and confusion and I had been knocked about rather more than a bit, but I was alive and kicking still though I couldn't have said for how much longer. Comrades Siezin and Kholov, however, were not despondent: the contact, they believed, would have been made in time. Maybe it had: we would find out in due course. I looked down at Smith's body; he hadn't done himself much good by his defection. I watched him being carried away to the cold store and wondered how long he would lie there with the food for the submarine's

188

company. As I had thought earlier, we might remain submerged for weeks; or we might move far to the south, down beyond the equator, looking for somewhere free of the fall-out. Or again, would Comrade Siezin risk it and make around the North Cape to enter Murmansk, or to lie perhaps for a while submerged off the Kola inlet as a very present challenge of Greenfly to the official naval command in case they should have ideas of remaining loyal to the Kremlin? I knew he would want to be in the vicinity if at all possible, ready to disembark and head with all speed for Moscow and the final takeover. If Greenfly had gone into immediate retaliation after the British missiles had landed, it was perhaps possible that only those parts of Russia that had taken those missiles would have been affected by the fall-out – the Russian missiles, so many of them available and ready targeted, could have obliterated the West's strike-back before it went into action at all.

I asked Siezin about this. "Yes," he said. "I believe so. I believe your country, and all the NATO countries, will be no longer viable. It will be very widespread."

I thought of London, of all the likely targets. I thought of the survivors, the still-fit ones desperate to get away, of a fearful exodus, perhaps, along the M1 for the north, a seeking of hideouts in the isolated areas of North York-shire, Cumbria, Northumberland, or west into north Wales. "You bastard," I said flatly.

He shrugged; he said nothing further to me but there was a conference with the submarine's captain and the vessel, which had lain stopped throughout Kholov's inter-ference routines, got under way again. The course, I saw, was westerly: out of the Skagerrak, into the North Sea. Which way would we turn from there – north or south? I reckoned we'd be unlikely to continue west for long, heading more or less towards the Firth of Forth and the patrol area where the *Iron Duke* had gone into her involun-tary firing.

As it turned out, we did head west for some while; and

189

then the course was altered to north-west and then north, presumably as we made around the butt of Norway, past Kristiansand and the Naze and up towards Stavanger.

So it was to be the North Cape and the Kola inlet: Comrade Siezin was impatient for world power. But, as time passed and another meal was brought, I began to sense something: I fancied Siezin was losing some of his confidence. There was a good deal of nail-biting and hurried, whispered conferences with Dr Kholov and the captain and Comrade Siezin's face assumed an anxious look. So did Kholov's, and the captain's.

Then I ticked over.

I laughed and said, "No signal – right? No Greenfly congratulations coming in along that trailing wire?"

"There is time," Siezin answered savagely.

"Is there, Comrade? I'd have thought – "

"Shut up," Siezin said. His temper was going fast now and his anxiety was clearly increasing. As for me, I was beginning to find a little hope: I met Felicity's eye. I believed she was feeling something similar. And it was just half an hour after this that a report came in from the sonar cabinet: there were engines in the vicinity, closing from the south and east. Siezin's mouth was set hard, his face had lost all its colour now. It was obvious that he didn't think those engines were Russian. Neither did I; only a matter of minutes after the sonar report there was a shattering explosion close at hand, then another and another, right and left and slap overhead. The submarine's hull rang like a bell and all the lights flickered madly, and then went out, all but one on the deckhead of the control-room. There was chaos, utter confusion, men shouting and running about like scared rabbits. Things fell about, metal becoming detached everywhere, and water spurted in under immense pressure. The boat took an upward slant, very fast and steep: there was a violent argument between Comrade Siezin and the captain. From a self-preservative instinct the captain, I gathered, wished to come to the surface pronto: with matters obviously gone awry he may also have wished to do what he could to re-establish himself with the official Kremlin leadership. Not so Comrade Siezin, who would be seeing the loom of Siberia or worse . . .

It was the captain who won out. His face livid, he drew a revolver. Siezin screamed out at him but the captain fired point blank and Comrade Siezin's face disintegrated into a bloody mess.

Within twenty-four hours Felicity and I were back in Focal House, closeted with Max himself, who'd lost track of both of us from the time of the abortive crossing near Braunlage – the wreckage of my Volkswagen had been found ultimately and had left a large question mark. Our journey back from northern waters had been by courtesy of the Danish authorities: it had been an escort group of the Danish Navy that had forced Siezin's submarine to the surface. I could still see the ring of armament and automatic weapons that had covered the Russians as the conning tower hatch had been opened up. The NATO chain of communications had worked with full efficiency.

Max said, "*Iron Duke*'s captain had noted some unexplained interference with his firing procedure. Your Dr Kholov, presumably. After that he decided to use his initiative, thank God – he surfaced and reported in defiance of patrol orders. His sonar, by the way, had picked you up – you weren't all that far off his submerged position." He gave me a thoughtful look. "D'you believe it would have worked. if you hadn't got Smith killed? *Was* it viable?"

I could only shrug. "I don't know. I think it could have been. But we'll never know now."

"Let's hope you're right! Anyway – the firing was inhibited in time, thanks to you. After that the word went out from Northwood . . . Danish co-operation was asked for, and the RAF Nimrods went into action with their

191

sonabuoys and pin-pointed you for the escort group." Max grinned. "The rest was easy enough."

I asked, "What about the Kremlin?"

Max grinned again. "What would you expect?"

I said, "Tight lips. Dead silence."

"Correct. A complaint about one of their peace-loving, harmless submarines being attacked, of course. But no explanations of anything at all. Obviously, there'd be a muzzle inside the USSR as well as externally. The ordinary comrades must never know what was planned. But I've no doubt we'll get some snippets through in course of time. I dare say we'll hear there's been a pogrom, a purge of Greenfly . . ."

I said, "It's those women I'm worried about. The Ladybirds. They'll be out on a limb now, even supposing they're still alive. We owe them everything, Max."

Max agreed, but didn't comment further. In this game, there were always the sacrificial lambs. I thought about Olga Menshikova and her girls in that lonely, snow-bound cottage, of all the people, men and women, who had helped to frustrate Greenfly. Of course the Ladybirds had been patriotic enough, had never acted against Russia, only against those who had wanted to force the Kremlin into war. But they had assisted a Western agent and a number of underground Greenflies might linger on, undiscovered. There would be bitter enmities and scapegoats would be looked for. But there was nothing I or anyone else in Britain could do about it. Only try to forget. Forget, and know that before long Max would be sending for me again with another mission in the offing.

I got to my feet and put a hand on Felicity's shoulder. I said to Max that I was going to get blotto and he nodded understandingly, making a gesture of dismissal. We left Focal House and picked up a taxi and went to a small drinking club off St James's Street where we could get a meal as well as drink. If we felt like it later, there was going to be a lot of work to be done on my flat.

192